Love and

Love and Gymnastics

Edmondo De Amicis

Translated by David Chapman

Hesperus Classics

Hesperus Classics
Published by Hesperus Press Limited
19 Bulstrode Street, London W1U 2JN
www.hesperuspress.com

First published in Italian as *Amore e Ginnastica*, 1892
First published by Hesperus Press Limited, 2011
Introduction and English language translation © David Chapman, 2011

Foreword copyright © 2002, The Estate of Italo Calvino
English language translation of Foreword © Andrew Brown, 2011

Designed and typeset by Fraser Muggeridge studio
Printed in Jordan by Jordan National Press

ISBN: 978-1-84391-193-7

CONTENTS

FOREWORD

On *Love and Gymnastics* by Edmondo De Amicis

'The house was well suited to intrigues and to the secrets of amorous passions': the space and the movement of the story are already given in this sentence. The passion of whose intrigues and secrets we are told is a passion for the feminine beauty, an athletic and domineering beauty – as in Wagner's Brunhilde and Baudelaire's giantess – of a teacher of gymnastics. This passion involves pretty much all the characters who have anything to do with her, but in particular a prudish, shy young man. The story is *Love and Gymnastics*, probably the finest, and certainly the most humorous, malicious, sensual, and psychologically acute story that Edmondo De Amicis ever wrote.

It was published, and I would be tempted to say concealed, in 1892, among the 'sketches and stories' of *Fra Scuola e Casa* (*Between School and Home*), one of the volumes in which the author performed his official duty as an anecdotal chronicler and cheerleader for the efforts that the new Italy was making to give itself a national identity, through somewhat dour institutions such as the army and the educational system. But in *Love and Gymnastics*, this little world appears to be fraught, a field of opposing forces between the idealistic impulses of the civil missions and the pathological entanglements of individuals and their secret lives. On the one hand, we have the atmosphere of fervour that drives the minorities of state officialdom, thirsty for technical information and new ideas (in this case the battle for gymnastics to be taught in schools: the cultural model is Wilhelmine Germany, another young nation, and a promising ally for Italy in the Triple Alliance);

on the other hand, the dense web of repression, unconscious erotic mythology, inner conflicts, and little perversions all smouldering away beneath the daily activities of the respectable subjects of King Umberto I.

Let us say straight away that gymnastics is talked about a great deal in the story, but not seen very much. We will wait in vain if we expect a writer of 'the visual world' such as De Amicis to take us to a gym or a sports field, show us gymnastic exercises, a trial run, a competition, some apparatus work, or a cycle race; in vain we will look forward to the gleams of historical colour that every old chronicle automatically gathers and transits to posterity. We find nothing of this, or almost nothing. A few rapid *faits divers*, a school essay by the 'Military Daughters', reach us indirectly, via people's conversations. Like a classical drama, the story preserves a rigorous unity of place: it all unfolds up and down the stairs of a housing block in old Turin, and in the rooms of three or four apartments. And when we eventually emerge, we find ourselves not in a gym, but in a national convention of schoolteachers, in the splendid halls of the Palazzo Carignano. (This description is a good example of De Amicis's journalistic skills.)

In *Love and Gymnastics*, gymnastics is above all an ideology. These pioneering teachers (already demanding to be called teachers of 'physical education' to avoid any lingering confusion with the kind of gymnastics you find in the circus) do nothing but talk (the two rival doctrines of Baumann and Obermann contend for supremacy), consult scientific treatises, hold conferences to spread their ideas, and write articles on 'Italy's ten gymnastics journals'. This is a gymnastics that seems to exist solely in verbal form – indeed, of the two most exclusive high priests of gymnastics that the story spotlights, the female schoolteacher Padani and the male teacher Fassi, the former can speak and write skilfully, and so triumphs; the latter has to rack his brains over every article or address, and feels frustrated and defeated. More than *Love and Gymnastics*, the title could be *Eros and Ideology*. Where lived experience is most keenly felt, it is all on the side of Eros.

Lithe, stately, impassive, the ideal beauty of the period, 'la Pedani' (we are never told her first name, and all the characters are called by their surnames, fathers as well as sons: the Italians of De Amicis are called by their surnames just as the class-members of the teacher Frossi respond to the school roll-call and the military roster), is endowed with a lush flesh all the more desired the more it is concealed ('If you saw her bare arm, you would agree that she has the most beautiful female appendage that has ever been seen under the sun,' is the first sentence in which she is introduced to us, and the story reaches its climax when, at a gymnastics lesson, she lifts up her skirt and 'he sees a flash of whiteness that flickered above her boots and blinded him as if it were a ray of sunlight'). Pedani has only to meet the male protagonist on the stairs and the narrative situation is established: he is skinny and self-conscious and dressed in black, while she, 'whether... on the step above or below, it always seemed that she towered over him like a colossus.'

The way in which De Amicis presents the young Celzani, known as Don Celzani because he is an ex-seminarian and always poses as a priest, but has 'a physical temperament that was extremely lively and a sensuality that was tightly controlled', is a real tour de force worth savouring. It is difficult to imagine a literary and dramatic commonplace more trite, more trivial (though its echoes are still found in the coarse Italian films of the present day) than the bigot in thrall to carnal temptation. And yet the irony of De Amicis is tactful, measured, quite unusually civilised; there is nothing complicit in it, and it is full of humanity and understanding.

And, at the same time, it is pitiless. What perverse potentialities are attributed to the Eros of this respectable young man! (But note that he is no longer an adolescent – he is already the wrong side of thirty.) Voyeurism (the keyhole is his normal channel of information, but he contrives to make a secret observatory for himself in a garret), visionary self-excitation (his reveries are effectively described as a rapid review of images), and fetishism (the inevitable boots), not to mention masochism…

Apart from having to defend herself from him – and from the assaults of the student Ginoni, who gets straight to the point and hardly bothers to stretch out his hands before jumping on her – Pedani is the object of another passionate relationship, a more shadowy one, so shadowy that perhaps even the author, despite being able to describe it in all its nuances, is not entirely aware of it. This is the relationship with another woman, quivering with femininity where Pedani is resolutely masculine: Zibelli, who lives with her, in a ménage of single women that has many characteristics of a marriage. Indeed, the story spells it out: when Pedani speaks to the other woman in her contralto voice, with its positively baritone resonance, 'if one did not know better, one would assume that she was a husband rather than a friend.'

They are a stormy couple, since Zibelli is fiercely jealous of Pedani, and the ups and downs in their relationship are the really variable element that motivates the linear development of the plot. How much this jealousy is really due to the fact that Zibelli is always falling in love with Pedani's suitors, and how much to the possessive affection that the more fragile partner nurses for her robust companion, impelling Zibelli to shield Pedani from the men who might take her away, can be left for the reader to decide.

We are left in no doubt, however, about every detail of the passion that delights the venerable master of the house, Commander Celzani, the uncle. His passion is for the feminine gymnastics of school gyms: a real spectacle and recreation for the eyes, the object of a contemplative rapture to begin with, and later of a daydream in which he fixes his dazed eyes on empty space; and the object, finally, of auditory pleasures when he hears the conversations, and the most innocent words such as 'movements' or 'combinations' unleash unmentionable associations of images within him. We would expect De Amicis to communicate such revelations about a white-haired notable of Turin (who is, to crown it all, a former member of local government involved in the school system), if not in the tones of a scandalised moralist, at least in the accents of someone saying: these are fine things to have to listen to! But no: he narrates it as the most tranquil phenomenon imaginable. Indeed, it can be said that what few gymnastic exercises the story shows us are seen through the hallucinations of the white-haired Commander, 'as if absorbed in celestial contemplation'.

Basically, gymnastics remains an elusive good, just like the teacher Pedani. For De Amicis, whether he considers it from the point of view of the old satyr's *esprit mal tourné*, or that of the pedagogic asceticism of the missionary teacher, gymnastics as discourse evaporates into the ineffable.

He is really concerned with only one theme: the stream of feminine energy that dominates the whole story. Right from the first pages, when the director of Turin schools refers to the crowd of three hundred schoolmistresses with whom he has to deal on a daily basis, we understand the vision that must have drawn – not without a certain dismay – the 'courteous captain'

Edmondo De Amicis to the world of education: that bound-less harem without a sultan, that warlike phalanx of women moving forward to attack, which spreads from classrooms and gyms like a swarm of armed Minervas from the head of Jove.

– *Italo Calvino*

INTRODUCTION

The northern Italian city of Turin is filled with history – not ancient history (although it is an extremely old community) – but modern Italian history. It was here that the contemporary Italian state was born, where its first parliament was held and where the Italian sporting movement first emerged. Unlike stately Rome, chaotic Naples or commercial Milan, nineteenth-century Turin was the Athens (or perhaps more aptly, the Boston) of Italy – a place foaming over with the sparkling effervescence of new ideas, liberalism and progress. It is little wonder that both the Risorgimento – Italy's movement to unify – and the sporting movement were born at roughly the same time and in the same place. It is also here that novelist Edmondo De Amicis has chosen to set his delightful novel *Love and Gymnastics* during the years 1879–80. The title tells the reader that this story will concern the pairing of two activities not normally associated with one another. Love is a common theme of novels, but why gymnastics?

From about 1850 until 1900, the most popular sporting activity in Italy was gymnastics. This fascination is all the more remarkable because gymnastics was rarely competitive; its aim was therapeutic rather than recreational, still Italians in their thousands participated in exhibitions of skill and athleticism rather than competitions. Italian athletes organised gymnastics clubs and societies and were spurred on by the aristocracy, who were not mere patrons since many members of the upper classes also participated in the activities. Eventually, this interest waned as other sports grabbed the public's attention and recreational activities became more class conscious; football was relegated to the workers and upper- and middle-class sportsmen preferred more decorous activities. However, the early interest in physical culture helped lay the foundations for a long-lasting fascination with sports at all levels of Italian society.

In the latter half of the nineteenth century northern Italy saw the growth of a solid and prosperous middle class that was similar to the bourgeoisie of many other western European cultures. Thanks to the development of railroads and the network of highways, it did not take long for European ideas to circulate among this burgeoning group. One of those ideas was that exercise was good for the health and another was that the individual was not fated to keep the physique that he was born with. It was in the dynamic and politically active middle class that the Risorgimento had its roots and financial backing, but after 1870 and the achievement of many of the goals of reunification, the bourgeoisie turned its energy and enthusiasm to other things, including sport.

Piedmont was at the forefront of many social movements, but one of the most important was education. In addition to feeding the minds of young Piedmontese, many progressives in the northern capital wanted to nourish their muscles as well. With the passage of the Casati Legislation in 1859 free public education became mandatory in all of unified Italy; this law also made 'Military gymnastics' a requirement in the institutes of secondary instruction. These were mainly group drills and light weightlifting, but they showed that Turin's Parliament recognised the importance of building a healthy and informed citizenry for the newly unified nation.

Despite the passage of the Casati laws, Italy did not immediately become a sports powerhouse; like most Europeans, Italians paid little heed to the culture of their bodies until the early twentieth century. This was largely due to two major conditions that were inherent in Italian society and which had to be overcome before it could be remade in Piedmont's image: in the rest of Italy, the middle class was small and there was little feeling of unity among the inhabitants of the various regions, so new movements were slow to spread across the nation as a whole. The other problem was Italy's oppressive poverty (especially in the south).

The problems may have been serious, but there was optimism, too. The nationalist writer Massimo d'Azeglio proclaimed shortly after 1870, 'Italy is made, now we need to make the Italians.' D'Azeglio and his countrymen were acutely aware that they were building a nation as well as a race of strong young people to inhabit it, and gymnastics became a political as well as a sporting act.

Into this heady mix, novelist Edmondo De Amicis drops a group of highly original and eccentric characters who simmer and stew in the Turinese urban cauldron. Like Rev. Celzani, the stolid, middle-class inhabitants of *Love and Gymnastics* are often portrayed as placid and reserved on the surface, but inwardly they seethe with half-understood passions and unfulfilled longings. It was this world of the Italian petty bourgeoisie that Edmondo De Amicis had been born into and knew best. De Amicis later maintained that he was merely an observer who jotted down what he saw. In a self-effacing summation of his career, he wrote, 'I am merely a journalist, one who takes note of everyday life and chooses from it a few typical episodes. Sometimes I enjoy entertaining my readers, but only to comfort them. I have no other ambition.'[i] But this is merely a wink at his readers; both sides knew that there was much more to the art of Edmondo De Amicis than simple reportage.

The author was born in the little Italian Riviera community of Oneglia on 21st October 1843, but his family soon moved to Turin where the author's father was the proprietor of a tobacconist's shop. Young Edmondo was a clever boy, and he wanted to attend university, but when his father became gravely ill, the young man was forced to enlist in the army and thus abandon his hopes for a university education and a literary career. Thus in 1863 De Amicis enrolled at the Military Academy of Modena and resolved to make a soldier of himself.

It was an interesting time to be a soldier in Italy because the peninsula was in a state of excitement over the great movement of unification known as the 'Resurgence' or Risorgimento that had captured the imagination of many Italians of all conditions, but particularly those from the middle and upper classes. As a young cadet, De Amicis was soon swept up in the patriotic fervour of the day, and in 1866 he took part in the battle of Custoza, an important skirmish in the so-called Second Risorgimento, which continued the unification struggle in the Austrian territories of northern Italy. Throughout his life, De Amicis would remain a passionate nationalist and supporter of the ideals of the unification movement.

In addition to fighting and serving his country, De Amicis was also continuing his writing career. He had published some early and very earnest verses on the subjects of freedom, love and other lofty topics, but his true calling was as a prose writer. In 1867 he began to write little pieces for the magazine *L'Italia Militare* in which he portrayed army life in a positive way and stated the importance of mandatory conscription of troops. The following year saw the publication of his first prose work, *Bozzetti di vita militare* (*Sketches of Military Life*) which was to undergo several additions and transformations until it eventually appeared as *La Vita Militare* in 1880.

After this brush with magazine writing, De Amicis resigned his commission and became a full-time journalist, at first for

L'Italia Militare, but then for other newspapers and magazines. On one of his assignments he was sent to Spain where he ended up staying for several months, and within a few years, he went to Holland, London, Paris, Morocco and Constantinople. The author had discovered that he had a talent for travel writing, and a string of books issued from his pen based on his travels to the various countries. De Amicis was unerring in finding interesting people, local celebrities and the spirit of the places that he visited, and he retained a lifelong love of travel.

By the mid 1880s De Amicis had a fairly substantial reputation as the author of military and travel books, but he longed to branch out into other areas; so in 1886 he published what has become his most renowned work, *Cuore* (*Heart*). Subtitled 'A book for children', this is an account of an entire school year told in the form of a schoolboy's journal (with occasional moral and patriotic stories thrown in for good measure) which became, for many Italian boys, a manual of conduct. It is a sweet and sentimental book full of realistic characters who must face circumstances that are both happy and sad, but its principal goal was to bring together young Italians in order to celebrate the same kind of nationalistic ardour that the author felt. The best place for this reconciliation was in schools and among the young who were Italy's future citizens.

Perhaps because of the great success of *Heart*, De Amicis discovered that he still had several things to say about education and the schooling of children, but this time the results were anything but a children's book. In 1890 he published a slightly disenchanted look at the teaching profession in his novel *Il romanzo d'un maestro* (*A Teacher's Story*), but it was not until 1892 that his most acerbic, sexually suggestive and maliciously amusing work was published in book form. *Amore e ginnastica* (*Love and Gymnastics*) was part of a group of novellas and brief sketches in the anthology *Fra scuola e casa* (*Between School and Home*).[ii]

Although *Love and Gymnastics* is now considered the best and the most famous of these novellas, it was not immediately clear that the book would become popular. Even the normally sanguine author was not very happy with the way it turned out. In a letter to a friend that was sent shortly after the appearance of *Between School and Home*, De Amicis advised his correspondent (a government official) not to waste his time reading the new book. 'It's not a book, rather it's a hodge-podge that I wish might pass unobserved and that I wish had not been published were it not that this year I have had a particularly nasty run-in with the tax collector.'[iii] Almost at once, however, readers showed that they held the book in much higher esteem than even its creator. Ironically, *Love and Gymnastics* was not the section that was singled out for the greatest praise. That honour was reserved for a sentimental work in the anthology called *La maestrina degli operai* (*The Little Teacher of the Factory Workers*), which was thought good enough to be published separately in 1895. It is easy to see why this story was so popular: it did not question any cherished values, it featured an upper-class school mistress who protects her honour and her virtue despite being pursued by an uncouth and lovesick ruffian nicknamed *Saltafinestra* (window-jumper) because as a youth he had jumped out of a window to escape the drunken rage of his father. Virtue triumphs and a deathbed conversion is brought about by a pure and simple maiden. How different it is from the other novella in the book, and how different from real life.

De Amicis was a great traveller and reader, and he must have picked up a few ideas from other writers of the time; most remarkable of these was the French novelist Honoré de Balzac.

The realism and interest in the details of the urban middle class must have inspired the Italian (although he lacked the Frenchman's scope and depth). Another quirk that both De Amicis and Balzac share is that they like to give some of their favourite characters a life in other separate works. The pedantic but loveable old Professor Padalocchi also appears in another brief story that gives his character a fuller development than as the wheezing old wreck in *Love and Gymnastics*. It is, however, Miss Pedani who is obviously the author's favourite character in *Love and Gymnasitics*, and she had already appeared in a work published two years before *Love and Gymnastics*, *A Teacher's Story*. Clearly, De Amicis had been reluctant to let the muscular young teacher go. She was much too original for him to leave her as a minor character; Miss Pedani deserved a fuller exposition.

Despite the successes of his literary life, De Amicis' private life was not so happy: in 1898 his beloved eldest son Furio committed suicide by shooting himself in the neck in a Turin park. The loss of his son caused a deep rift to open up with his wife, and the writer was never quite the same afterwards. Financial reverses and the death of his wife in 1900 caused a further breakdown in his physical and mental state. Finally on 11th March 1908 Edmondo De Amicis died of a cerebral haemorrhage at his home in Bordighera not far from his childhood home. To the end of his life, De Amicis had remained one of Italy's most beloved writers, a witness to his country's unification as well as the rising prosperity of its middle class. With the changing values and economic status, he still retained a healthy sympathy for the working classes. It was this mixture of benevolence and patriotism that endeared him to the Italian public. Finally, in October 1923, on the eightieth anniversary of his birth, the people of Turin erected an impressive statue and monument to De Amicis in the park across from the main rail station. At its dedication hundreds of schoolchildren filed past the statue while waving flags, carrying bouquets and giving the Fascist salute.[iv]

The principal reason for this outpouring of affection was the one great book that had remained in print and in the minds of his countrymen – *Heart* – and gradually most readers forgot the other works that De Amicis had written. He was remembered as a simple writer of travel books and children's novels, but all that changed in 1971 when the great Italian novelist and critic Italo Calvino rediscovered *Love and Gymnastics*. Calvino immediately saw the startling erotic possibilities that the novel had presented to its nineteenth-century readers, and he was determined to bring this work back into the light. His enthusiasm is apparent in the introduction to the novel that accompanied a new edition of the book. He announced that *Love and Gymnastics* was 'probably the finest, and certainly the most humorous, malicious, sensual, and psychologically acute story' that the author ever wrote.[v] It was unlike almost anything that De Amicis had ever produced before, but because of the author's prolixity, the novel's brilliance had been buried under thousands of less lustrous pages.

Calvino's view is that the dark, mysterious house set in the middle of a respectable Turin neighborhood is itself one of the most important players in the novel. 'The house suited itself well to intrigues and secrets of amorous passions,' writes De Amicis, and the rest of the novel bears out this judgment. Doors open and close, characters spy upon one another and overhear private conversations; they encounter one another and generally spend many important moments coming and going in the stairway. It is a gossip's paradise. So much occurs on the stairway of the apartment building that this would have been a very different book indeed if the Commendatore Celzani had decided to install a lift.

The entire building pulses with women and their power, and this is a concept that Calvino notes quite clearly. 'The current of feminine energy dominates the entire story… that boundless harem without a sultan, that warlike phalanx of women moving forward to attack, which spreads from class-rooms and gyms like a swarm of armed Minervas from the head of Jove.' The building itself is a former convent: further confirmation of the important role that women will play in the story. It is eventually clear that the dark, seductive stairway in fact represents the eternal female principle – a vagina symbol – that exerts its sway over the puny and helpless men who scramble up and down its steps.

This view of powerful womanhood is very much at odds with the prevailing culture of nineteenth-century Italy. As a strongly masculine, Latin society, Italy was not exactly at the forefront of women's rights. The Pisanelli Code of family law was formulated in 1865, and it declared that women were under the direct control of the male head of household; once they were married, they had no control over their children and could engage in neither commercial nor legal agreements without the consent of their husbands. This was backed by the reactionary stance of the Catholic Church; in 1880, the exact year that *Love and Gymnastics* takes place, Pope Leo XIII issued the encyclical *Arcanum*, which emphasised woman's role as wife and mother who was supposed to maintain a modest and compliant demeanour at all times. The last thing that Italian society seemed to want was a cadre of female physical culture teachers romping around the gym-nasium filling girls' heads with foolish and possibly indecent ideas.[vi]

Neither the Italian government nor the Pope had counted on two irresistible forces: the first was the desire of many women to free themselves from the social bonds that constrained them and the second was the sporting revolution that was sweeping the western world in the late-nineteenth century. With the growth of industrialisation and the move away from agrarian economies, workers gradually gained a few hours of free time. Sport seemed like a perfect way to fill it up again. Although the upper and middle classes had discovered the joys of physical exertion many years previously, it was only in the late 1800s that the movement caught on among all social classes in northern Italy.

Actually, sport is not a proper name for the craze that struck post-Risorgimento Italy: the great reigning passion of Italy was rational, educational gymnastics. It might seem odd for an entire nation to devote itself to vaulting, balancing and calisthenics, but there was logic behind this seemingly bizarre choice. Italians had been divided into separate often antagonistic states for centuries, and after they had finally been joined back together, it seemed absurd to pit one patriot against another, so sports on the Anglo-Saxon model were seen as divisive and dangerous. What better way to celebrate the recent unity of all Italians than by exercising in unison, by participating in a uniquely Italian activity and (most importantly) by promoting harmony rather than competition. It would not take the nation long to grow out of this situation, and Italians like other western European cultures soon became as competitive as everyone else, but at this time in its history, physical exercise, nationalism and morality were all joined together in the gymnasium.

That unity was promoted in physical education, but it did not mean that the sport was devoid of controversy. One of the most virulent of these controversies in the early years of Italian sport was the great divide between the two gymnasiarchs, Obermann and Baumann. This debate adds considerable spice to the narrative of *Love and Gymnastics*, and it is impossible to fully understand the novel without some appreciation of the two philosophies.

The first stirring of the gymnastics craze arrived in Turin in 1833. In that year a Swiss athletic instructor came to Turin in order to teach gymnastics to the Piedmontese army. His name was Rudolf Obermann, and his arrival in Piedmont signalled the beginning of modern, physical education in the Italian peninsula. In terms of Italy's sport history, however, Obermann's greatest triumph came in 1844. In August of that year the Società Ginnastica di Torino was founded. As early as 1839 Obermann had been approached by various young men who wished to have private lessons from the Swiss master, and the number of pupils who came from outside military circles continued to increase over the years until eventually, it became feasible to create a civilian organisation completely independent of the Savoyard army. Obermann began to publish his routines and philosophy of exercise, especially for the instruction of the young. His most famous work was *The Manual of Equipment for Educational Gymnastics*, which appeared in 1865. Despite his interest in gymnastics for the young, Obermann's name was forever linked to the military work that he had so ably pioneered; his goal was seen as turning young men into sturdy soldiers for the fatherland. His methods were also seen as foreign importations from the Teutonic north.

In contrast with Obermann's Germanic methods was another system of gymnastic exercise that was championed by Emilio Baumann. In 1877 Dr Emilio Baumann had founded a new teacher-training school in Bologna in order to help turn out more gymnastics instructors for the Italian school system, but as he grew more adept at both instructing and physical education, he determined that the Obermann method needed some adaptation to the Italian situation. Eventually, Baumann compiled a new system of gymnastics based partly on the Swedish system of Per Henrik Ling, partly on the work of Obermann and partly on his own experience. Baumann used the nationalistic fervour then extant by calling his new amalgam 'Italian gymnastics'. These new exercises were meant to be 'natural'; by this Baumann meant that he emphasised walking, marching, climbing, jumping and other body movements. This had the added advantage of not requiring special equipment or apparatuses, as did the system of Obermann and others. It was clearly these Italian gymnastics that appealed more to De Amicis, and he supported them for several reasons: it was simpler, more rational and nationalistic. It is also less militaristic than other forms and more beneficial to ordinary schoolchildren.

De Amicis had a genius for translating the issues of the day into flesh-and-blood situations, and in *Love and Gymnastics* we have both a human and a theoretical drama that plays out in the streets and inner corridors of Turin. In essence the book is a cautionary tale on the problems of gender, strength and weakness. Fortunately, there is enough humanity and humour in the book to save it from being an artless tract or a shrill political diatribe. Italo Calvino suggested that a better title for this book would have been 'Eros and Ideology' because of its unusual mixture of theoretical gymnastics with the steamy passions and amorous intrigues that lace its pages. As historian Suzanne Stewart-Steinberg explains, 'Celzani falls both into love and into ideology,' and if he wants to win Miss Pedani's love, he must accept the theories and values that are so sacred to her.[vii] The athletic theories derived from the writings of the two giants of Italian gymnastics, Obermann and Baumann, form the philosophical centre of the novel and are constantly quoted, debated and bickered over.

Maria Pedani, the fictional heroine of *Love and Gymnastics*, considers Baumann a hero. She will not allow anyone to defame him or even to joke about him. Naturally, De Amicis exaggerates her worship of this gymnastics teacher to the point of being humorous, but the respect that he receives is palpable throughout the novel. Even Baumann's personal eccentricities are imitated by some of the lesser characters. Fassi, the hapless gymnastics instructor, abruptly ends his conversations or brusquely switches subject in order to make himself seem more like his idol. Unfortunately, Fassi has none of the great man's talent or intelligence, and he remains a pale imitation of this saviour of Italian youth. It is Miss Pedani who embodies all the real 'Baumannism' that Fassi lacks. Despite the favourable light that shines on Baumann as opposed to Obermann, the controversies between the two philosophies ignite many of the verbal fireworks in the novel. From today's perspective, however, the arguments between the two philosophies have all the relevance of Byzantine theological controversies that were once taken in deadly earnest but are now little more than historical footnotes.

If this novel were simply about a minor movement in Italian sport history, then it would make a clever comment on the past, but not be very interesting from a literary perspective. Fortunately, that is not the case. If the novel did not feature such sympathetic protagonists, the book might have remained a witty but forgotten opus from a very prolific author. For example, the 'Reverend' Celzani is presented as an eccentric but likeable character. Dignified and careful, Rev. Celzani is only thirty years old, but he is described as having the bearing of a man of fifty; he dresses in black, continually keeps his eyes lowered and holds his interlaced fingers on his chest as if he were forever fingering a rosary. Celzani is certainly not impressive from a physical standpoint – far from it – but it is the inner life of the man that intrigues both the reader and De Amicis. The little man dressed in quasi-clerical darkness resembles the blue-bleak embers in the poem by Hopkins that are sombre on the outside but that 'gash gold-vermilion' when they burst open. The author takes great pains to describe Celzani's character as being highly sensitive but basically dissatisfied with extra-marital sex because that alone could never fulfil his deepest desires; Rev. Celzani is condemned to seek his ideal woman because only she can gratify his longings and his physical desires. As we are told, the smokescreens of passion do not deceive the drab little secretary; his longings can only be quelled by possessing 'a unique, reliable, honest and unblemished object of affection'. Compromise is out of the question for him.

Fortunately, De Amicis has arranged that the long-sought ideal is living in the same apartment building as the secretary, but thanks to the author's malicious sense of humor, the woman is Celzani's physical opposite. Where he is small, slightly bent and physically weak, his paragon is tall, athletic and superbly beautiful; although her nose is a trifle large, her voice a little too husky and her gait a bit manly, this does not seem to detract from her strikingly original appearance. She attracts admirers who are drawn to her loveliness and her unique blend of masculinity and femininity. She has the same effect on people in the little town of Camina in the earlier work, *A Teacher's Story* (1890). The author notes Pedani's disinterest in making herself look conventionally pretty: 'The only refinement of her coiffure were two curls that fell onto her forehead (a habit from girlhood), but which she did not always remember to make, and sometimes, because of haste, if she did them at all, they resembled the handles of a shovel.' We are told that the teacher is certainly not unsociable, and that as soon as the ladies of the area had got over the initial shock of her amorous conquests, they noted that she did nothing to encourage the men, and thereafter the women were nearly as seduced by her originality as their sons and husbands. As for her self-enforced celibacy, the ladies had two principal theories: either Miss Pedani had a fiancé in some distant place to whom she was unswervingly faithful, or she was completely immune to love. While she was in Camina in *A Teacher's Story*, however, only the sergeant of the *carabinieri* vainly persisted in following her around and arranging to encounter her 'accidentally'.[viii] All this comes to an end when Miss Pedani moves to Turin where the events of *Love and Gymnastics* would soon take place.

Although Maria Pedani is consistently portrayed as strong, muscular and incisive, she is also a caricature of nineteenth-century athleticism gone mad. Miss Pedani is as brilliant intellectually as she is physically; she writes articles, eloquently debates the merits of gymnastics and gives stirring speeches to adoring throngs. Her scholarship in her chosen field is beyond reproach, but like the man who adores her, Miss Pedani is obsessed to the point of blindness and impotence. She sees nothing of the greater world around her; she can do nothing but improve and encourage others to convert to her worldview.

The real subject of this novel is how obsessions can isolate us from our fellow human beings and cut us off from the most important things in life. Rev. Celzani is obsessed with winning

Miss Pedani, and he nearly ruins his life in that pursuit. Miss Pedani is consumed with her love of gymnastics, and that almost destroys her chances of real happiness. Love and gymnastics, the twin subjects of the title, are also the things that torment and isolate the two main characters. Celzani goes a little mad when he realises that he can never possess his ideal, and he alienates everyone around him. By the same token, Pedani finds herself isolated by her stubborn resistance to outside influences; she quarrels bitterly with her only friend and finds herself admired but alone. Rev. Celzani learns to be a 'man', to build his muscles at the gym and to show a little of his fiery inner passions, while Miss Pedani learns to be a 'real woman' by compromising a few of her virile qualities.

This novel is unlike others in many ways. In fiction, at least at this time, it was usually the woman who pined with love and the man who was bold, athletic and insensitive, but thanks to the impish humour of De Amicis, the roles have been reversed: it is the woman who represents the flesh and the man who symbolises the soul. More than this purely intellectual exercise, *Love and Gymnastics* is a work that is highly unusual for its time for one other reason: its amazing candour about the various quirks and peccadilloes that are enjoyed by the characters. In fact, it would not be too much of an exaggeration to say that the book is a virtual catalogue of sexual diversity.

The list starts with the Commendatore and his trance-like fantasies, which apparently involve watching little girls jump around and display their lithe bodies for the old man's delectation and titillation. The engineer Ginoni is aware of the landlord's peculiar interests and reveals them to Miss Pedani, but even after she knows of the man's attraction to young girls, she clearly indulges his passions and invites him to an exhibition at the Institute of Military Daughters. Perhaps she considers his paedophilia an innocent and harmless fantasy, but another explanation is that she enjoys tormenting helpless men.

Old Celzani is not the only one who takes pleasure in watching pretty girls from afar; his nephew is a far more confirmed voyeur. Rev. Celzani is continually stealing glances of his beloved through the keyhole, watching her go up or down the stairs or following Miss Pedani in such a way that modern readers might call his actions 'stalking'. De Amicis describes his hero as he listens to the movements through the ceiling of his bedroom, picturing the scene in his overheated imagination as the young lady takes off her clothing and strews it around the room prior to getting into bed, or as she sweats and strains with her dumb-bells. Celzani takes his voyeurism to its logical extreme when he climbs into the dusty attic so that he can spy on the gymnastics teacher while she is giving lessons to her young charges. He is rewarded with a glimpse of her leg, and like the original Peeping Tom, her dazzling white skin briefly blinds him.

It seems clear that Rev. Celzani is tormented, but he also rather enjoys the delights of masochism. He continually refers to himself as being Miss Pedani's servant or slave; he denigrates himself and looks forward to the time when she will make him grovel under her lovely but brutal heel. Is Miss Pedani innocently unaware of her effect on the poor little man, or does she have some inkling of her effect? She gives him an encouraging smile, she talks gymnastics with him, and seems to goad him on while at the same time keeping him at a distance. No wonder Celzani nearly goes mad from the strain induced by this stately dominatrix.

Miss Pedani is a curious creation. She inspires sexual desire in other men, but she never seems to return the sentiments:

'She who wounds but cannot be wounded,' as Ginoni describes her. Perhaps she secretly enjoys the havoc that she inspires; in *A Teacher's Story*, the author goes to some pains to explain her neglectful appearance, but when she arrives in Turin at the end of that novel, Pedani meets the main character wearing 'a tobacco brown suit that was tight as a glove and which attracted everybody's gaze'.[ix] Is she really *that* unaware of her effect on passers-by, or is she a closet exhibitionist? There are other questions about her motivations that are even more perplexing. Pedani claims that she must remain celibate because of her pure and holy devotion to gymnastics, but that cannot be the entire explanation. There are many hints in the text of Pedani's odd relationship with her friend Miss Zibelli. Their bond is described as a sort of 'marriage' with Pedani playing the traditionally masculine role and Zibelli as a fluttery and foolish feminine partner. Even Italo Calvino was intrigued by the relationship between the two women when he commented on Miss Zibelli's rages directed at her roommate's putative beaux. 'How much this jealousy is really due to the fact that Zibelli is always falling in love with Pedani's suitors,' he says, 'and how much to the possessive affection that the more fragile partner nurses for her robust companion, impelling Zibelli to shield Pedani from the men who might take her away, can be left for the reader to decide.' In the end, the only thing we can do is to agree with the engineer Ginoni who philosophises, 'A girl is always a mystery; the only thing you can do is to trust her face and the feelings of your own heart.'

Ultimately, there are many questions that must go unanswered, but there is little doubt that Celzani and Pedani have reversed the traditional gender roles. It is true that both characters have edged nearer to the traditional sex roles that

Italian society revered, but no matter what might happen, Pedani never seems able to surrender her usual 'masculinity'.

It is perhaps this 'dark paradise' of muddled sexuality and jumbled gender roles into which Celzani is dragged by the powerful and beautiful object of his affections. This is a paradise that comprises not only the mysterious realm of physical love, but also the inner reaches of another human soul. Like the dark staircase in the Commendatore's house, this is the mysterious cave of love where the varied and shadowy elements of two people's souls make all things possible.

– David Chapman, 2011

Notes on the Introduction

i. Quoted in the introduction to Giorgio de Rienzo's edition of *Amore e ginnastica e altri racconti* (Milan: Rizzoli, 1986) 6.

ii. According to Bruno Traversetti in his *Introduzione a De Amicis* (Rome/Bari: Laterza, 1991) 95, *Love and Gymnastics* is meant to be the reverse of the educational medal for which *Heart* is the more palatable side.

iii. From an unedited letter quoted in Giorgio de Rienzo's introduction to *Amore e ginnastica*, 7.

iv. *La Domenica del Corriere*, 4 November 1923.

v. 'Nota introduttiva' to *Amore e ginnastica*, originally published in the 1971 edition of the novel by publisher Einaudi, Turin. All further quotations by Calvino are also from this introduction.

vi. Information about the status of women in nineteenth-century Italy can be found in Gigliola Gori, *Italian Fascism and the Female Body: Sport, Submissive Women and Strong Mothers* (London: Routledge, 2004) 37, 44.

vii. *The Pinocchio Effect: On Making Italians* (1860–1920), (Chicago: University of Chicago Press, 2007), 172.

viii. *Il Romanzo d'un Maestro* (Milan: Treves, 1906) vol. 2, 94–95.

ix. *Il Romanzo d'un Maestro*, vol. 2, 257. This is perhaps the same simple, brown dress that Maria Pedani wears to the great Congress at the end of *Love and Gymnastics*.

Love and Gymnastics

At the corner of the via dei Mercanti the secretary tipped his hat formally to the engineer Ginoni, who answered him with his usual, 'Good morning, my dear secretary!' Then he took the via San Francesco d'Assisi to return home. It was twenty minutes to nine o'clock, and he was almost certain to meet the one he was expecting on the staircase.

Ten steps from the front door he bumped into the moustachioed gymnastics teacher Fassi on the pavement, reading press proofs; Fassi stopped for a moment, showed him the papers and said that he was in the process of correcting an article on the horizontal bar that his colleague, Miss Pedani, had written for *The New Arena*, the gymnastics journal for which he was one of the principal editors.[1]

'The report is well done,' he added. 'I only have to touch it up here and there. Ah, now Miss Pedani is one of the finest exponents of the art of gymnastics. Mind you, I don't say that she is a master of the art of writing – after all, we can't do everything well. But then, as we all know, in the science of gymnastics, a woman's intelligence only goes so far… But as a practitioner, she is without equal. It is true that Mother Nature formed her for it; she has given her skeletal proportions more perfect than I have ever seen – a thoracic cavity that is a revelation. I observed her just yesterday doing a bust rotation as an experiment. She has the flexibility of a ten-year-old child. And the artistic gentlemen come to me claiming that gymnastics deforms the fair sex! She handles dumb-bells like a man, and if you saw her bare arm, you would agree that she has the most beautiful female appendage that has ever been seen under the sun. Good day to you, sir.'

In this way he brusquely ended every discourse in order to imitate the famous Baumann, 'the great gymnasiarch', as he called him, who was like a god to him.[2] The secretary grew pensive. Without realising it, that ranting master Fassi had tormented him for some time with all the details of the teacher's strengths and beauties, which he already thought about too much. Just then those two images of the rotating bust and the bare arm caused his nervousness to increase, but this always happened when he mounted the stairway hoping to meet his neighbour.

He climbed the first stairs with slow and silent footsteps, straining his ears, and when he was on the first landing he heard above him the sound of footsteps, and he felt the blood rise to his cheeks. The two teachers, the Misses Pedani and Zibelli, descended together, as they usually did to go to school. He recognised the contralto voice of the former.

When he found himself face-to-face with them halfway up the second flight of stairs, the secretary stopped and lifted his hat, but instead of looking at Miss Pedani, he was overcome by timidity and looked (as he always did) at her companion, who (also as usual) believed herself to be the cause of his agitation, and encouraged him with a fond smile. And then they held one of the usual stupid little dialogues that happened on those occasions.

'You're leaving for school so early?' he stammered.

'It's not as early as all that,' Miss Zibelli answered sweetly. 'It's nearly quarter to nine.'

'I thought it was eight thirty.'

'Our watches are more accurate than yours.'

'That might be. It is foggy this morning!'

'Fog comes before good weather.'

'Sometimes... we can always hope. And... it is a pleasure to see you again.'

'Goodbye.'

'Goodbye.'

Reaching the head of the staircase, the secretary quickly turned just in time to steal a glance at Miss Pedani's beautiful shoulders and mighty arm, but at that very moment Miss Zibelli, without her friend's noticing it, turned to him and beamed a smiling gaze.

Right then and there he made a resolution. No, he could not continue in this way; the foolish figure that he had once more cut in her presence had given him the final impetus. He did not think it possible to survive further with that torment of physical desire that he encountered every day because he could not even bring himself to look at her. He had made up his mind: he would send the letter that had been lying for a week on the little table. He wanted a sentence of life or death.

Arriving at the second floor, he opened the door with a forceful movement and went directly towards the room of his uncle, the Commendatore Celzani, landlord, so that he could hand in the rents from the other house in Vanchiglia and then go immediately afterwards to reread for the last time the letter that must decide his destiny.[3] But a short distance from the door he heard two voices in the room; he stopped and put his eye to the keyhole. He saw together with his employer a rather short and fat man, with a face that was broad, beardless and wrinkled, like an ageing boy who had suddenly swelled up; the man wore a small, black wig that lay sideways. He had known him for a considerable time. It was the superintendent of the municipal schools, who passed by via San Francesco on his way to the office, and who sometimes stopped by to greet the Commendatore, with whom he had been on terms of intimate friendship for eight years, since his uncle had been an assistant alderman in charge of public instruction. Nonetheless, the secretary, who had become suspicious of everyone ever since his secret amorous passion had developed, started eavesdropping at the door, supposing that they were speaking of him. He calmed down a little after hearing that the director was speaking, according to his custom, of the great and delicate difficulties of his own position regarding the concerns of the teachers.

'You understand,' he said in a slow, asthmatic voice, 'they go to give lessons in noble families; they know about things that pass between the deputies and the senators, sometimes they deal with high functionaries in the Ministry. It is important to be careful. Certain of them are even supported by His Majesty's household. You can stir up a hornets' nest before you know it. It is a duty (as you are well aware) that requires tact and a delicate touch that so few have. It requires nothing less than taking charge of a family of 250 to 300 ladies – some of them young, some not so young, married women and widows, coming from all social classes, not to mention a cadre of directors who… well, it would be easier to manage thirty princesses of the house of Hohenzollern. You cannot imagine the worries that it gives me – what with their loves, illnesses, marriages, honeymoons, examinations, pregnancies, rivalry, conflicts with superiors and relatives… Believe me, there are times when I feel like banging my head against the wall.'

And they continued to talk in generalities. After reassuring himself thoroughly, the secretary retreated a short distance to wait. As soon as the superintendent had gone the secretary entered the office of his uncle, who still sat in his armchair, wrapped in his dressing gown with his serious and soft blue eyes staring at the ceiling as if he were absorbed in celestial contemplations. After the secretary had given an account of his doings, the young man put the bank receipts on the side table. His uncle made a sign of approval with his handsome white head, as was his wont, and wordlessly turned his eyes once more into the distance to do more thinking. The secretary then tiptoed out, entered his room and took out from a locked drawer a four-page letter written in perfect calligraphy. He reread it with deep attention, put it back gingerly in the envelope and attached a postage stamp with great care. He went out without letting anyone hear him and went to the corner of the street; after hesitating a little, he raised his hand in front of the letter-box and let the letter fall in. Then he breathed a deep sigh. The die had been cast. There was nothing left to do but to leave things to God.

Secretary Celzani was only a few years past his thirtieth birthday, but he had the bearing and behaviour of a man of fifty – like a notary in a comedy or a tutor in the house of a conservative patrician. An orphan from boyhood, he had been raised by a maternal uncle, a village priest who had brought him up in the sacristy and then put him in a seminary to make a priest of him. But then the priest died, leaving him a little money, and the young man left the seminary and moved into the house of his Uncle Celzani, a childless widower, in order to be a secretary and administrator of his holdings in the country, a responsibility he fulfilled with both honesty and a truly exemplary zeal. He went to church, kept company with priests, and from the priests picked up certain mannerisms and attitudes such as often clasping his hands over his breast, having an aversion to moustaches and beards, and habitually dressing in dark colours. But he was no bigot, and he could boast without lying that he was a patriot and a liberal. Nonetheless, because of his appearance all the tenants of the house had for years called him 'Reverend' Celzani in jest.[4] And while they found in him a slight tinge of ridiculousness, they respected and liked him since he was polite and helpful and timidly respectful of everyone equally. When his patience had been put to the hardest test, he had no more resentful exclamation than 'Great God!', which he said as he lifted his eyes heavenwards and extended his arms wide as if in an act of invocation.

But there was a side to Celzani's nature that nobody knew. Under that priestly disguise was concealed a physical temperament that was extremely lively and a sensuality that was tightly controlled (not by hypocrisy but partly by timidity and partly by a sense of decorum), which was concealed from most people under an air of profound meditation. He was unimpressive when seen in the street: a man attired in black, a bit stooped, with dark, flowing hair, with a beardless face, with two eyes that were so small that when he smiled they disappeared completely, and with the long, slender nose of an ascetic. He walked with a seemingly studied gait that made him look small and with a gaze that was always pointed downwards and about ten paces ahead. No one would ever have guessed that not a well-turned foot glimpsed on the steps of a carriage, nor a slightly risqué photograph in a shop window, nor a pair of spooning lovers in a doorway, nor any other picture or object that might excite the senses would escape his notice. His temperament only revealed itself in his large, mobile mouth, made up (as one might say) of two little vermilion serpents, or in the sudden blushes that made his neck and face flash red for a moment after thinking certain thoughts. Undoubtedly, the blessed soul of his priestly uncle would not have been able to follow after him everywhere; but his behaviour was so dignified and prudent that even those who knew his habits best would not have discovered anything that would make them suspect that he was anything other than what he seemed to be. After all, his was one of those natures that was not vulgar in its sensuality; it was one that disdained vice simply because vice could not satisfy him, and which could find its satisfaction only in possessing a unique, reliable, honest and unblemished object of affection. Natures that are amorous rather than sensual, natures that wait and seek, that are restrained without a great deal of effort – if these natures do not find the incarnation of a certain physical and moral ideal that smoulders in their hearts, then they are more difficult to satisfy than others who are colder and more refined – they are not deceived by the smoke of passion.

Rev. Celzani had at last found this ideal in the teacher, Miss Pedani. She was originally from Lombardy and had arrived three months earlier, at the beginning of December, and lived with her colleague Miss Zibelli in rooms on the third floor of that house across from Professor Fassi's front door. The editor had put her there so that he could better assure himself of her valuable cooperation in *The New Arena*.

That tall and strong lass of twenty-seven, 'wide of shoulders and narrow of waist', was of statuesque proportions, breathed health and strength from her entire body and would have been extremely beautiful if her nose had been a little finer and her facial expression and gait a bit less manly.[5] From her very first appearance, she had exerted on Celzani the effect of a person long wished and waited for. She was the sort of girl that he had caressed in his overheated dreams when he was at the seminary, the same type that he had confusedly contemplated with pleasure for the entire course of his ardent and tortured youth.

The first time that he entered her home was to collect the rent for the next quarter, but he had not been able to count the five lira notes lined up on the chest of drawers. From that day his passion had increased and grown warmer. And as soon as he had understood from her behaviour that she had a robust, unflappable character that was repugnant to every flirtation, that she hardly noticed the impression produced by her own presence and that she gave no hope to either humour or whims, his thoughts forged ahead and he resolved to propose marriage as the only possible way to achieve the satisfaction of his desires. Despite his ardour, he foresaw the difficulties that he could reasonably expect to come from his uncle's opposition to his marriage to a gymnastics teacher who lacked both family and fortune. He was hopeful that the 'no' would not be absolute because of an unusual passion (the only one that he knew of) that the Commendatore seemed to have: an extremely active spirit for advancing educational gymnastics, which he had promoted in every way during his brief tenure as deputy alderman in charge of education. He had withdrawn from those activities, but he retained a lively and constant sympathy for all gymnastic spectacles at schools, colleges, institutes and academies, and he never missed a single one of these, being one of the first to be invited to all of them as one of the founders of the Turin Gymnasium.[6]

It was precisely this love of gymnastics that had made him reduce Fassi's rent (whom he had met at the gymnasium many years earlier) by a third. He had accorded the same favour to Miss Pedani, who was a gymnastics instructor in various institutes and was noted for the efficacy of her teaching and for her lively little articles in the athletic journals. The secretary thought that the same feelings that had made him lower the rent to a tenant would make him reduce his opposition to a bride. No, the most terrible difficulty was not from this quarter; the most terrible was daring to declare his passion openly to her. Thanks to his invincible timidity, this was an act that he had postponed for three months – a timidity that was caused essentially by the unfavourable comparison that he established between the young lady and himself on the basis of their respective outward appearances. Since he knew the precise times of all her lessons, he had arranged every day (and sometimes many times during the day) to go out or return home at those exact moments in order to meet her on the stairway and to open his heart to her. He had met her a hundred times, but on none of those occasions had he been able to get out of his mouth anything other than the most ordinary and insipid words. It did no good even to prepare himself in advance with the first sentence, to down hastily two little glasses of Caluso wine or to seek courage in the assurance that his intentions were honest. Whenever he found himself in front of that tall, strong girl – whether it was on the step above or below (it always seemed that she towered over him like a colossus) – all his temporary boldness collapsed, for the most part without his even daring to lift his gaze from her beautiful waist or her stupendous shoulders all the way to her face.

He was probably not even successful in making her guess his own passion, since he was so calm, with always the same nonchalance typical of a young man when he greeted her and she spoke to him. And so he lived, ruminating on his love, every day adding the excitement of a new image to an interminable collection of poses, vocal sounds, movements and wriggles, which he would then keep in his head and pass continually in review, meditating on them one after the other with increasing voluptuousness and torment that gave him little peace. In the end he could stand it no longer, and he wrote the letter.

The house suited itself well to intrigues and to the secrets of amorous passions. It was one of the oldest houses in Turin, a former convent, so it was said; without attics, without balconies on the courtyard, with only two ill-lit stairways. There were only six apartments off each of these stairs, and most of them were rather small and inhabited by quiet people. On the level of the landlord's office – the first floor – lived the engineer Ginoni with his family. It was with these people that Miss Pedani had been connected since she was the teacher of one of the little daughters when she was a pupil at the Margherita School.[7] On the same level there were two elderly and wealthy sisters; they were dedicated to the church and were punctilious to the point of never raising their eyes to look a man in the face; all the same they were very pleasant. At first they greeted Miss Pedani, but stopped saying hello to her later because they learned from the servants that she was taking a class in anatomy and physiology applied to gymnastics conducted by Dr Gamba.

On the second floor, directly across from the commendatore, lived an elderly professor of literature, a certain Cavaliere Padalocchi.[8] He was a widower and a pensioner who was said to be a formidable linguist but was extremely well mannered. He sometimes accompanied Miss Pedani in the stairway talking to her about his illnesses.

The third floor was all scholastic and gymnastic, and the two apartments were undoubtedly the oddest in the house on account of the life that was led in them. The two teachers were the main reason for this peculiarity, and this was because of the great differences in both their natures and their habits. They were so different that it seemed odd that they had decided to live together. Miss Zibelli was thirty-six years old and was the physical opposite of her friend. She was just as tall but thin and narrow of shoulder; a pretty face, but too small and already faded; she lacked the obvious contours of a shapely body. Thanks to the taste with which she dressed and her way of throwing out her feet energetically, it was understood that her knees were friends that were a little too intimate. She must have been rather charming in appearance; she once had very beautiful chestnut hair, and her greatest glory was to have been in love at the Domenico Berti School with a young professor of physics who blushed whenever he asked her a question, but the glory was faded, and her hair had thinned. The bitterness of a long maidenly life for which she had not been born had put two sour wrinkles in the corners of her mouth and a murkiness in her eye that revealed a soul in torment. Even this would not have been too bad, but an irritable and inconsistent humour spoiled everything. She had formed a friendship with Miss Pedani on moving to the neighbourhood, and she soon began to feel like an older sister to that big, beautiful, careless girl who was heedless of herself and of domestic things and with whom she shared an enthusiasm for gymnastics. This common interest drew them together and suffocated with affection the pangs of jealousy and envy that she felt for her friend's opulent beauty. It was for this reason that she had proposed that the two set up house together, and they had lived together thus for two years. But the growing familiarity soon bred a little contempt. The first discord had been born the year before, on the occasion of the Great Gymnastics Congress in Turin in which the two divisions arose between the Obermann or Baumann schools.[9] Miss Pedani was firmly dedicated to the latter, which was more strenuous, and Zibelli remained with the former because it was more feminine in nature. Then other disagreements had arisen from more serious causes.

Miss Zibelli was constantly in love and had an incredible facility for believing that this affection was returned. All it took was the smallest act of courtesy by a colleague, a superior or a relative of one of her pupils, and in a sudden flight of fantasy she discovered (or so it seemed to her) a surge of affection between her would-be lover and her beautiful friend that diverted his attention from herself to Miss Pedani; it was undoubtedly unintentional, but it was precisely this that caused even greater irritation. And then followed unpleasant times during which she could not stand her friend and quarrelled with her interminably if a lamp was out of place, if it were taken away too soon, if she arrived late to the table – for all the most frivolous pretexts. She was irritated even more by finding that none of her anger made even the slightest impression in Pedani's healthy mind, which resided in her healthy body, in which quick and hot life circulated. It seemed that her continuous and happy industriousness suffocated all notions of the little disagreements of her home life. Then Miss Zibelli took a fancy to someone else, and as long as the illusion lasted, she returned to the expansive and protective friendship of the early days, helping to dress her, teasing her about her messiness, almost delighted by the admiration she saw others give her. But conversely, if disappointments happened (as she believed, because of her friend) the demonstrations of her acrimony would become stronger and of longer duration. When she was in one of these periods, she did not accompany her friend to school any more, spoke ill of her to the neighbours, went the entire day without opening her mouth or argued all day. But she never succeeded in making her angry. In the discussions the friend agreed with her when she was right and reasoned calmly in the contrary case, not giving importance to anything other than to the basics of the thing, and when Zibelli had been pouting all day, she contented herself with looking at her every now and then out of curiosity as she went about her own business very naturally. She was unchangeable in her 'manly' friendship, without tenderness and without fantasies that gave much and demanded little.

The last rupture had been caused by the instructor Fassi, who had inspired in Miss Zibelli a warm affection. She had been severely vexed by the continuous conferences on gymnastics with Miss Pedani, and she would have made good her often-stated promise to leave the house if force of habit, the remnants of good will and not having some overt excuse had not kept her there. But more than anything else, she had by then acquired the opinion that the secretary had fallen in love with her. And not only did she remain in the house, but her friend and she had returned to their earlier tenderness.

But Miss Pedani had not even paid this much mind. She lived with one thought alone: gymnastics. It was neither ambition nor amusement that motivated her, but the deep conviction that educational gymnastics, if diffused and performed as she and others intended it, would result in the regeneration of the world. She had always been attracted by this discipline because of her masculine temperament, which was opposed to any softness or mawkish sentimentality in education – so much so that in student registers she would inexorably cross out all the nicknames and would allow only the most common given names that had been consecrated in the calendar of the saints. After the new impulse given to gymnastics by Minister De Sanctis and the powerful propaganda of Baumann, her passion had increased and had obtained for her a certain notoriety in the Turinese scholastic world.[10] In addition to teaching in the female section of Monviso, where she was also on the regular faculty, she taught at the Margherita School, the Institute of Military Daughters, the Soccorso Institute and to the children of Gymnasium members, extending to all under her instruction the vigorous emotion of her own enthusiasm.[11] She truly seemed to have been born for this one role in life. She had succeeded in performing for her own pleasure the most difficult, manly exercises on the horizontal bar and parallel bars. Thanks to her scholarship, she had also succeeded in becoming an incomparable theoretician. Miss Pedani was also admired by all the experts for her rare quickness at varying the exercises for which she herself had devised all sorts of combinations. She was remarkable for the unusual vigour of her command, which made the movements quick, easy and instantaneous, as well as for the extreme acuity of her vision, which never missed the smallest irregularity of comportment – even those that were performed in the most crowded rows of pupils.

She was taking a course in anatomy at the gymnasium at that time, but she had already studied the subject with great diligence, accompanied by much reading two years earlier; she was thus able to modify and base her instruction on a more than mediocre understanding of the human organism and hygiene. She knew how to recognise at first glance whether a girl had a talent for gymnastics or not. She examined the deformations of the body, searching out asymmetrical shoulders, protuberant chests, prolapsed abdomens and knock knees; she then devised ways to correct each defect with an appropriate regimen of exercises. She dedicated herself to this task with a maternal zeal, striving to persuade the mothers (when they were reluctant) of the effectiveness of her method. She waged an implacable war against busts that were too narrow and against clothing that was too tightly laced; she kept records of the stature and weight of certain pupils to verify the results of her care. She had purchased a dynamometer with her own money to measure their strength, and she had denied herself a few little things in order to buy a device to measure pulmonary capacity.[12] She would have loved it if someone could invent mechanisms to measure the beauty of comportment, dexterity, the faculty of balance – everything.

Aside from her lessons, she occupied herself with specialised technical problems, by attending various regional meetings of gymnastics instructors, by recording their deliberations, and by reading those foreign works on the subject that had been translated and which happened to come to hand. She never missed a single issue of any of Italy's ten gymnastics journals – for most of which she was a correspondent. One of her articles on the practical utility of jumping, written gracefully and with strength, had aroused the admiration of the instructor Fassi, and brought about their friendship, a relationship that was profitable from Fassi's point of view since he was bursting with ideas and knowledge of the subject, but to tell the truth, he was as devoid of style and grammar as the Marshal in the play by Émile Augier.[13] Miss Pedani made up for his deficiency quite well, converting his notes into articles at the bottom of which Fassi boldly signed his own signature. But Miss Pedani cared little about this, for she did not write for glory. She was completely dedicated to her schools, constantly rushing off to the four corners of Turin; studying at her desk when she was not running around, busying herself with gymnastic experiments when she was not studying her books. She worked indefatigably on her calling for the physical regeneration of the race, not heeding the thousand stares that were elicited by every turn of her beautiful body nor the envy and jealousy that she aroused. This quality was so pronounced that those who knew her well considered her a unique female character who was completely impervious to love and virtually devoid of the sexual instinct. Engineer Ginoni, who enjoyed joking with her, called her 'She who wounds without being wounded.' It seemed that she justified this opinion in regards to her attire, with which she took little or no care except to make sure that it was spotless, but in this it was irreproachable. She would leave the house one day with her hat askew; on another day her coat would be unbuttoned or she would wear the wrong boots. When she walked, her strides were much too long, and when she spoke she allowed the tones of her masculine voice to escape causing people to start and turn. And when she rolled her r's for a particularly long time, it resembled the high-pitched croak of a tree frog. But none of this mattered. All these defects (not to mention her long nose) did not detract a bit from the mighty and triumphant beauty of this young Amazon.

Miss Pedani and Miss Zibelli shared both a maid and a large room that was used as a parlour. Miss Pedani's room was on one side of the parlour and that of her friend was on the other; these rooms were as different from one another as were the natures of the two inhabitants. Miss Zibelli's was kept very neat; it was decorated with little pastels painted by her in earlier times, with a profusion of crochet work, with flowers made from paper and leather, lampshades, knicknacks and playthings all made with her own hands. There were several little shelves here and there covered with embroidered curtains in which school books rubbed up against numerous French novels that, according to experts, should be strictly prohibited at school, since in pedagogy as in an intellectual monastery one either forgets the world and its temptations or one throws one's whole soul into the reading of fantasies.

In Miss Pedani's room, however, it was just the opposite. There was always a confusing disarray resembling that of a second-hand dealer: clothes strewn here and there, gymnastics blouses with dark stripes hanging from nails; in a corner there was a Jäger Stick, two pairs of dumb-bells under the bed, exercise clogs at the foot of the wardrobe, and scattered around almost everywhere were issues of *The New Arena*, *The Field of Mars*, *The Padua Gymnasium*, *The Belgian Gymnast* and other journals of the same ilk.[14] At the head of the bed next to a torn school calendar there hung an inscription in calligraphy of two lines by Parini in a gilt frame given to her by her students:

What can stop a daring soul
If the body's strong and whole?[15]

Her library consisted of a pile of unbound volumes on a table covered by a newspaper; it was a collection of every sort of gymnastics manual: handbooks, atlases, manuals of rhythmic gymnastics, brochures on hygiene, swimming and cycling, as well as publications of the Alpine Club; her passion for gymnastics clearly embraced all the physical disciplines that human beings are capable of. But the thing that gave the oddest aspect to the room was the great number of portraits, most of which had been taken from illustrated newspapers, that were attached to the walls like in a print-seller's shop. Aside from Baumann (who was in a place of honour) there were the most famous Italian gymnasts: Gallo of Venice, Pizzarri of Chioggia, Ravano of Genoa; above all of these were

Ravenstein, the Nestor of German gymnasts; Firmin Lampière, the 'steam-powered man'; a photograph of Bargossi; a reproduction of an oil painting of Ida Lewis, decorated with the gold medal from the Congress of the United States for having saved shipwreck victims; and about ten others.[16] This topsy-turvy shambles served her as both bedroom and office – not to mention as a gymnasium and schoolroom, since every day as soon as she arose, she did her exercises there and gave her private lessons there. It was also a second parlour for the two women, because when they were both in a good mood, Miss Zibelli was attracted by the oddness of the disorder, and she would come in constantly to have little chats with her friend.

They were both at home precisely at seven o'clock in the evening after having dined. Miss Pedani was seated at a little table illuminated by a kerosene lamp skimming a book by Dr Orsolato on gymnastics using the rings as Miss Zibelli, who had passed her arm around her friend's shoulders, gazed idly at her.[17] It was then that the concierge brought the letter from the secretary.

Miss Pedani asked the lady to come in so that she could repeat once more the warning she had been giving her for a month: she should stop torturing her child. The woman had said that her daughter was acquiring a spinal curvature, and she allowed herself to be persuaded by the proprietor of an orthopaedic supplies dealer in the neighbourhood to put her in a corset with metal stays that squeezed her ribs too much and caused the child to suffer and to wail like a banshee. Miss Pedani wanted the mother to throw the thing out since it might well cause pulmonary consumption, and entrust the child to her for a gymnastics cure. But the mother did not believe her, and once more gave her the usual answer, 'Ah, Miss! If gymnastics were the only thing she needed!'

'I pity you,' replied Miss Pedani.

After the concierge had left, she looked at the address on the letter, but she did not recognise the handwriting. Miss Zibelli got up as to leave, but the uncertainty of her steps showed that she had little desire to depart, and Miss Pedani invited her to stay. For her part, Miss Pedani had no secrets from her or anyone else.

After opening the envelope, she looked at the signature and began to read without giving any indication of wonder. It was only after she had finished that she smiled and shook her head while staring at the page, as if this were the first time that the various signs that would have allowed her to anticipate this situation had been made clear.

Miss Zibelli was tormented by curiosity, but she held back because of the other's silence, and she did not dare to ask. Instead, she watched her friend out of the corner of her eye as she arose and carelessly threw the letter in the drawer of the desk, then Miss Pedani went to the wardrobe and got her hat. Miss Zibelli remembered that her friend had to go to the Alpine Club to attend a lecture by the Countess Palazzi-Lavaggi on 'Mountaineering by Women'. Just then an idea came to her, but to ward off any suspicion, she said smilingly, 'Oh, you have your little mysteries.'

'It's no mystery,' replied Miss Pedani indifferently, 'I'll tell you about it later,' and she carelessly jammed the hat on her head.

Joking lightheartedly, Miss Zibelli accompanied her to the door, then she went to make sure that the maid was in the kitchen; she quickly re-entered her friend's room and grabbed the letter in the drawer. When she saw the signature, she turned pale. She then read the entire letter and was seized by such a storm of anger that she looked around, filled with a temptation to break and stamp on everything. She had stolen even him! Oh, the cursed creature! Just then she could have riddled her with a thousand pinpricks. And the thing that enraged her the most was that although there was no mention of marriage, it was understood however by the almost comic gravity of every sentence that it was not a declaration of love that was made casually and with simple gallantry as its purpose; rather, it was a carefully planned and difficult letter to write, the results of a passion that had grown for a long time and which had a serious intent. She had been able to delude herself in that way and had served as an accomplice to both of them!

She slammed the letter back in the drawer and paced around the room two or three times, but she felt as if the air in the room would suffocate her. She needed to get revenge at once, so she gave her hair a little adjustment and left the rooms. She crossed the landing and knocked on the door to Mr Fassi's apartment, doing her best to put a pleasant expression on her face.

Fassi's wife opened the door with a scowl on her face because she had expected Miss Pedani, but seeing her friend instead, she relaxed and had her enter a small room with bare, white walls in which four little boys were making a hellish racket around a half-set table in the middle of the apartment. Miss Zibelli knew that she was certain of finding in Mrs Fassi an ally against Pedani (whose familiarity with her husband bothered her more than she cared to say). She was a woman in her forties with breasts so enormous that they hindered the motion of her arms; she had a large mouth almost devoid of lips, and she went around the house dressed like a common labourer. It took her three quarters of an hour to go up or down the stairway since she stopped to talk in her whiny voice to whomever she met, and particularly with the secretary, who was up-to-date on everything thanks to her. She was particularly jealous of her robust thirty-eight year old husband, and it seemed that she had some sort of appreciation for the coarse beauty of his inflexibility, which consisted of nothing more than the boldness of his attitudes and his thick moustache, which extended from ear to ear. But she also feared him, and because of this she dared not be openly rude to her rival.

Miss Zibelli said that she had just wandered over for a little visit, and she pretended to be cheerful, patted the children and wandered about the room waiting for the right moment. The time seemed right when Mrs Fassi asked her if she was home alone this evening.

'Yes, alone,' she replied. 'Maria has gone out. Besides, she no longer cares about me. She has quite another thing on her mind.' And noting Mrs Fassi's curiosity, she could no longer contain herself, and with the forced tone of a joke, she told her of the secretary's love, but without mentioning the letter. The woman's mouth dropped open: the thing seemed unbelievable to her. Then she said, 'How do you know?'

'I know,' the teacher answered.

'But… to marry her?'

The teacher made a gesture as if to say that there was no doubt.

'The secretary is mad,' said Mrs Fassi with poorly concealed annoyance. 'But… what about her?'

'For the moment she feigns indifference,' Miss Zibelli replied. 'But she will eventually say yes ten times in a row.'

'Pooh!' the lady exclaimed. And after a moment of reflection, 'Mr Celzani will have second thoughts about it.'

'Well, what do you *want* Rev. Celzani to think?' Miss Zibelli shouted, aware that she had planted a seed in fertile ground.

She carelessly threw out a few words that the other one harvested and stored up in the deepest part of her memory.

'Rev. Celzani is inexperienced. To him a girl of thirty and one of fifteen are all the same. Since he is ignorant of the world, he thinks that everyone else is ignorant, too. I'll bet that he doesn't even know that before coming to Turin she had been a teacher in half a dozen towns, and,' here she began to laugh, 'the adventures of village teachers are well known, even the newspapers have reported about her. There was the story about a company of soldiers, of all things! Oh, there are strange things that go on in this world!'

Carried along by her anger, she was on the verge of saying something even worse, when the doorbell began to ring loudly. The boys were immediately silenced, and the lady ran to open the door, and Professor Fassi entered excitedly grasping *The Turin Gazette*. He had just returned from Chieri where he went twice a week to give gymnastics lessons at the high school and the technical school.

He barely greeted Miss Zibelli, when he turned to his wife showing her the newspaper that he squeezed in his fist. 'Do you want to know the latest news? Some ass of a dancing master is attacking me in an article in *The Turin Gazette* because in last week's *New Arena* I stated that dance is merely a *branch* of gymnastics. What is it that they don't understand? I have done them an honour that "the art of the pirouette" doesn't deserve. I will deal with you in another article; you'll see how I demolish this fancy "staggering" that you call *dance*.' And he continued to declaim, planning the article while pacing back and forth in the room.

'It is high time to demonstrate clearly the errors of these ignoramuses. They do not see a single difference between a teacher of gymnastics and a circus acrobat. Good Lord, a gymnastics master is a man of science! He has to know theoretic gymnastics, applied anatomy, pedagogy, hygiene, the history of gymnastics, the construction of equipment and gymnasiums, and technology; *and* he must be an artist! Stupid asses, don't they know that it takes an entire lifetime to learn and remember these exercises? Why, you could write a hundred volumes on the installation of the equipment alone. But then look what a professor of gymnastics is reduced to!' And he extracted from his pocket a sheet on which a professor of mathematics from Chieri had researched by means of algebraic formulae the number of changes of position used while exercising with wands.

This was his great ambition: to make gymnastics as complex and difficult as possible – for himself as well as for others. Unlike Miss Pedani, Fassi had no ideals about the good of humanity; he loved his science for the satisfaction that he found in it and for the hope that it gave to his pride. Other than at Chieri, he taught at the high school and technical school of Carmagnola, at a grammar school and a high school in Turin, at the Crafts School and at the Gymnastics Society, and everywhere he attempted to inculcate his ideas. 'The first nation of the world,' a great man had said, 'will be the one that possesses the best health – in other words, the one that performs more gymnastics.' And he added, 'To this science, therefore, we must gather all the energies of great geniuses, of governments and all of society; this must be put above all the sciences. The teachers of gymnastics will become the nation's elite.'

Until that happened, Fassi sought fame and recognition. He frequently mulled over a number of different ambitions, the principal one being to invent a piece of exercise equipment that he could name after himself.

And then he went back to the dancer, reproaching himself for having profaned the name of gymnastics by speaking of dance, just as he had been profaned by professional acrobats who had appropriated that name. He then launched into an attack against the government, which, despite the appeals formulated by the Gymnastics Federation during its second conference, persisted in its refusal to prohibit circus acrobats from vituperating against science. They would have made great strides forward if they had adopted, as he had suggested, the appellation of 'Physical Instruction'. Then he brusquely asked, Baumann-like, 'What's new?'

His wife blurted out what was new: Rev. Celzani wanted to marry Miss Pedani, the teacher. But after saying this, she did not see the expression of jealousy in her husband's face that she had expected. In fact, he did not feel for Miss Pedani anything except the admiration that a mechanic feels for a beautiful machine, and he had never thought of her except of how she might serve him in fulfilling his own ambitions. He was sorry, nonetheless, to hear this news because he could foresee that afterwards she would escape from his clutches, and he would be left without an editor. But he did not express this thought. Instead, he said, 'Madness! A true gymnastics teacher should not take a husband; she needs to be like a soldier, free in body and soul. Miss Pedani should dedicate herself completely to her mission. And her mission is not to produce children; it is to cure the children of others. She won't be so stupid. I will persuade her.'

Then he asked suddenly, 'How is it that this plaster saint had the nerve to fall in love with such a beautiful girl?' Mrs Fassi made a few tentative suggestions about beauty; she thought for example that Mr Celzani was much more distinguished than the girl. And then Miss Pedani was a young lady who was devoid of feeling – that was clear to all. Miss Zibelli also made her comments, 'She has a nice waistline; that's all. After all, she may have a certain fineness of features, but she is too big; she lacks grace. In the house she runs into everything. She stomps around like an elephant.'

The teacher shrugged his shoulders, 'All that counts for nothing. Miss Pedani was not meant for the likes of him, not to mention the fact that he is an idiot, and she is a talented girl.'

'Talented!' his wife exclaimed. Turning towards Miss Zibelli, she said, 'My husband must correct her articles.' Miss Zibelli knew the truth of the matter, but she smiled and looked as if she believed her. She said gravely, 'She knows nothing of syntax. She rambles.'

'This is true,' observed the teacher. 'Frankly, as far as journalism is concerned, it would be better if she contented herself with a more modest role that would put her less in the public eye. There are some matters in the field of gymnastics that a lady cannot and should not deal with. But in the end Mr Celzani will not marry her, you'll see. I'll put a flea in his ear. I know how to get rid of overgrown altar boys.'

The doorbell interrupted him. It was Miss Pedani returning from the Alpine Club, where the lecture had not taken place after all, and she came to fetch her friend. She came into the room and chose not to sit down. She was flushed pink by the bracing evening air, and she was breathing a bit deeply, thus dilating her nostrils and heaving her wide breast. Her figure in black stood out against the white walls in such a bold and striking form that Mrs Fassi had to turn and shout at the boys in order to destroy the silent admiration caused by the sight of her.

'I've come to take you home,' she announced to Miss Zibelli, putting such an emphasis on the last word that if one did not know better, one would assume that she was a husband rather than a friend.

Miss Zibelli stirred and exchanged a few words with her hosts, and they both departed. Miss Pedani was the last one out, and for a moment she filled the void of the half-open door with her beautiful shoulders.

'All things considered,' said the teacher as he continued to stare at the door after she had gone out, 'it would not seem that Rev. Celzani has his head up his backside.'

Smiling astutely, his wife added, 'He's not married her yet.'

The secretary was distressed and uncertain all that day and the morning after; should he wait for a reply to his letter or should he take courage and ask her in person? He concluded that he should be courageous, and he knew that at quarter to two on Sundays she went out alone to go to the gymnasium, so he positioned himself behind the door to his apartment and peered through the keyhole waiting for her to appear on the landing. If anyone had seen him in that position, Celzani would have been mistaken for a man waiting to commit a murder since his entire body was quivering and he was breathing heavily. A noise startled him, and he darted his head out the door, but he soon pulled it back; it was only old Professor Padalocchi, bent over and wrapped up in his big fur coat, coughing as he went out for his daily constitutional. But a moment later he heard the footsteps of Miss Pedani. Great God! The opportunity was lost. The teacher reached the old man's landing, and he greeted her enthusiastically, and she stopped and spoke with him. Every word of their conversation fell like an enormous weight on the poor man's lovesick heart.

Mr Padalocchi complained of a new inconvenience: he had trouble breathing.

'Why?' Miss Pedani asked him. 'Don't you do pulmonary gymnastics?' The old man smiled, but she persisted. 'I'm serious. There is nothing better for dilating the chest. Every day after rising you must try to do several deep breaths... like this.' And she did them, causing a rush of blood to the secretary's head.

'Do ten or twenty of them at first,' continued the teacher. 'And then add a few every day – ten more if you can. I assure you that at the end of two weeks, you'll feel much better. It's an exercise of guaranteed effectiveness. Every morning I myself do one hundred and thirty of them.'

The old professor seemed convinced and thanked her.

'Try it,' repeated Miss Pedani, 'and tell me about it afterwards. And then I will lend you a book that contains all of the theories. Good bye.'

This said, she continued walking. The secretary hoped that he would be able to discern a glimmer of her mind from the way she looked at the door of his home while passing in front of it, but she went by without looking at the door. He was dismayed. Nevertheless, there was still time to intercept her at the front door of the building, if nothing else he might question her with his eyes, but as he launched himself out the door, he heard someone shouting in his face. 'Oh, my dear secretary!' Great God! It was the engineer Ginoni, who had come as he did every year to ask his old friend the landlord to come down that evening for a small, family get-together that he was accustomed to give on the birthday of his twins.

The second attempt had failed. There was nothing left but to await his sentence by mail.

There were only a few people in Ginoni's home that evening. Professor Padalocchi could not come, Miss Zibelli did not want to, and the landlord had not shown up. In the dining room a large oval table was covered with fruit, sweets and bottles of Sardinian and Sicilian wine; around this stood only the family, Miss Pedani, three of the daughter's little friends and their grandmother who lived in the other wing of the house. But the young people who were in the majority at the get-together gave to it grace and happiness, forming a lovely crown of blond heads under the warm glow of the rich gas lamp which gave a golden quality to everything. The little girl (who was still a pupil of Miss Pedani's at the Margherita School) was thirteen years old and seemed to be an exact copy of the smallest boy, who was her twin and a student in the middle school.

The eldest son, Alfredo, was a twenty-one-year-old student of mathematics at the university and an ardent cyclist. He was a cheeky young rascal with blond hair and two beautiful but malevolent eyes that were already as shameless as those of a man who had seen a good deal of the world. He had contrived to sit so close to the teacher that she had been forced to move back a little in order to avoid rubbing up against his shoulder and hips. He was the apple of his mother's eye. This lady was not yet forty years old. She was elegant, indolent, thin as a rake and graced with a large aristocratic nose; she was perfectly nice so long as one did not run up against the blind love that she felt for her son.

The most sympathetic member of the family was the engineer, a handsome man of about fifty years; he was grey-headed, good natured, hard working, a great talker, great joker and a lover of the finer things in life, but he was without pretension. The husband and wife had a cordial liking for Miss Pedani partly for the respectable originality of her character and partly because their little daughter adored her; they did not dissent with her for that despite a declared aversion to gymnastics that had been caused years before by a nephew of theirs who was a pupil at a boarding school in Milan and who broke his arm when he fell from a climbing pole.

'We're friends,' Ginoni was accustomed to tell her when he met her on the stairway, 'but only until we reach the doorway of the gymnasium,' or, 'Down with gymnastics!' and every time he encountered her, he teased her facetiously like that. And the conversation ended there (as it did that evening). In order (among other things) to criticise the new teaching methods, the engineer told her about having seen the previous year a performance of rhythmic gymnastics by the Institute of Military Daughters at the institute of San Domenico where he had gone to visit.

'Yes, the show was enjoyable. One hundred and fifty husky girls in those pretty black and blue uniforms with the little white aprons, all lined up in a vast courtyard and moving in unison at the command of an instructor with the graceful motions of a contradance, while making a rhythmic rustling sound that seemed to be whispered music. All those beautiful arms and tiny hands in the air, those big braids falling on rosy necks and on slender torsos, three hundred slender, arched feet, and the indefinable grace of those movements somewhere between dancing and leaping. And those long dresses gave them the appearance of a chaste *corps de ballet*.

'It was new and seductive without a doubt! But, good heavens! What a number of words issued from that teacher in order to make them move – more words than movements! They were the endless commands of a brigade general ordering an exhausting and complicated choreography. And furthermore, the movements are confined and measured off in centimetres, so insufficient for these well-developed bodies that are so full of life. These are combinations of measured exercises that have been scribbled down with a pen in order to create a show for competition judges and their guests.' If it had been up to him, the 'performance' would quickly have been cut in half, and they would all have been led out into a flowery meadow to gambol around like a herd of young fillies.

But on this point Miss Pedani was in agreement with him. She was a Baumannist because Baumann detested choreo-graphic gymnastics and preferred a more manly philosophy.[18]

'Well, then,' said the engineer, 'I must insult Baumann if I am to make you angry.'

'I will defend him,' the instructor replied, 'should you try!'

'No,' he said, smiling. 'I won't do it. I am not encyclopedic enough because gymnastics now embraces all the sciences.' He quoted a lecturer at the Philotechnical Society, which he had attended a few evenings ago for an explanation of gym-nastics; he had first made a wide romp through philosophy, ethnology and anthropology, and had then turned all of human knowledge upside down; after that he had ended with dumb-bells.[19]

'Gymnastics,' replied Miss Pedani quietly, 'has a relationship to all of science.'

'And how could it not?' responded the engineer. 'It is more-over the key to everything. Now they say that a boy who en-counters difficulty in solving a mathematical problem must only do a quarter hour of exercises on the parallel bars, then he returns to his desk and the problem is solved.'

'The engineer is joking,' said Miss Pedani, shrugging her shoulders. 'I will not reply any further.'

'I'm not joking,' Ginoni insisted (continuing to jest). 'Is it not also said that gymnastics will replace medicine entirely? It seems to me that Professor Fassi has written that there are certain exercises that are the equivalent of certain medical prescriptions. Odd fellow, that Professor Fassi! I believe that it was also he who found some marvellous transformations in the musculature of his students from Monday morning to Saturday evening. For example, he has an extremely original idea for society: people hopping down the street, saw-horses and parallel bars in every square, obligatory wrestling in all offices, upper body exercises in home parlours…'

'Say no more, sir,' said Miss Pedani, 'because it pains me to hear a man like you making light of a thing that is so serious. How can one joke about gymnastics so long as we call up three hundred thousand recruits, eighty thousand of whom must be rejected because of physical weaknesses? While we have secondary schools full of pale young people who have the chests and arms of babies, and when out of ten girls from the best society, we cannot find two without some constitutional defect! Oh, it's a pathetic joke, indeed!'

'I beg you to forgive me,' replied the engineer. 'I have no quarrel with gymnastics. The gymnastics that I am speaking of is this new scientific-literary-apostolic-theatrical gymnastics that they have invented in order to have festivals and performances, to manufacture big men, to increase the number of shows and to wiggle the tongue and the pen a thousand times more than the arms and legs. I hardly think that it is *this* gymnastics that the lady defends.'

'I do not defend it,' she replied, 'because it doesn't exist; it is nothing more than an invention of its creators. I only know rational gymnastics, founded on the knowledge of anatomy, physiology and hygiene, which gives strength, agility, grace, health and good humour to childhood and which raises all the moral and intellectual faculties. I believe in these effects because they are proven, and I have seen them; I therefore believe that gymnastics is the most useful and the most sacred of educational institutions for our youth, and those that attack it – please excuse me, Mr Ginoni – give me much pain; to me they seem to be blind, unwitting enemies of humanity.'

The engineer chuckled a little at the light declamatory tone of the last words. 'No, Miss,' he then said, 'I am not an enemy of humanity. I am an enemy to those who without consulting a doctor (which should always be done but never is) force gymnastics on boys and girls who have maladies and deformities, and who injure them. Do you understand me? I am equally the enemy of those who devise selfish rivalries between the strong and the weak which result in the breaking of the weak one's neck. I am an enemy of those who reduce gymnastics (which should be a balm to the spirit) to artificial theories that occupy and tire the mind as much as any other study. And I am also an enemy of exaggerations. I believe that the good effects of gymnastics are undeniable, but they are absurdly exaggerated, thus deceiving everyone. Permit me to assure you, for example, that I am firmly convinced that no exercise or gymnastic appliance, could have produced the blooming health and the harmony of form that you see in your wardrobe mirror.'

The elder son showed his approval by clapping his hands. The glimmer of a smile flashed in Miss Pedani's eyes, but she quickly became serious again. 'It's always like that,' she responded. 'I give some reasons, and he replies with jokes. I will only say this: Germany and England, which are the two most powerful nations in Europe, are those that perform gymnastics the most. The Greeks, who were the most powerful people in antiquity, were the most athletic people in the world, and,' she added with a smile, 'as you well know, in order to avoid rebellion among the inhabitants of Cumae whom the Greeks had subdued, Aristodemus prohibited them from doing gymnastics.'[20]

'They probably did it to make friends with them,' replied the engineer.

The teacher remained silent for a moment, and then said with vivacity, 'Luckily, not everyone thinks as you do. You are ignorant of our world. The concept that we support is gaining credence everywhere, even in Italy. Do you not know that there are hundreds of gymnastics societies? That there are men of conviction who have dipped into their patrimonies in order to found gymnasiums, that there are a great many young doctors who have dedicated their entire studies to gymnastics. That there are hundreds of teachers who learn foreign languages just so they can study gymnastic literature from around the world that numbers thousands of volumes and which has been written by eminent scholars?'

The engineer made a vague sort of gesture without answering, because he had been busy for the last few moments making signs with his head at his elder son, who stood so close to the teacher and stared at her with a smouldering intensity that was downright indecent.

'Down with Baumann!' he said finally, just to break the silence.

But when it came to Baumann, Miss Pedani would brook no jesting. She attacked! Baumann was the benefactor of the nation; he was the founder of a new gymnastics that would have borne great fruit – a great genius, a great scholar, a moulder of character. She had met him at a convention of gymnasts: he was the perfect example of a man destined for great things. Although he was nearly sixty, he seemed to be a young man; he had a superb forehead. He made lightning-like gestures, uttering an incisive word with the dominating eloquence of a soldier and an apostle. If he had been given the means, Baumann could have remade the nation. The women of Italy should have erected a statue to him if for no other reason than for the reforms he wanted to make to female gymnastics.

The engineer fluttered his hand while doing a pirouette. Mrs Ginoni took up the argument with her indolent voice, 'And yet, my dear young lady, gymnastics for ladies has its disadvantages, too. Dance instructors observe that it impedes gracefulness and habituates one to unseemly movements. It is the same with piano teachers; they say that when girls return from the gymnasium they no longer know how to play. Drawing masters also complain of it.'

'Professional jealousy,' Miss Pedani answered. 'You may believe it, madam. It is impossible that gymnastic exercise works at cross purposes with dance or any other art since the observed effect of exercise is that the synovia flows more abundantly in the articulated joints of the bones and makes all movements easier and freer. Do you not see? Even your young son agrees with me. By the way,' she added, turning toward the young man, 'I must thank you for your beautiful gift.'

The young man gave a start, but did not blush. All the same, he would have preferred silence. With studied casualness, he announced to his mother that (guessing the teacher would like it) he had given her the floor plan of a Greek gymnasium that he had copied in the library.

Mrs Ginoni smiled wanly and then said to Miss Pedani, 'Last Sunday Alfredo won top honours in the cycling races.' Miss Pedani made him tell all about it. She was greatly interested in those competitions; she knew the names of the usual winners, and sometimes she went to the track; despite this, she had never actually been on a conveyance of this sort. She spoke of large-wheeled velocipedes, tricycles and bicycles with a thorough understanding of the subject. But this time, as he told the adventures of his race in which he had waited chivalrously for a fallen competitor to get up again, the young man drew so near to her, flirting shamelessly, that his father could do nothing more than to make an angry gesture, but the boy never saw it.

'So you see,' remarked the teacher to the engineer as she moved her chair back, 'even your son is on our side. The majority of us in this house are thus in favour of gymnastics: Mr Fassi, my friend and me, Mr Padalocchi who does pulmonary gymnastics, your son, the Commendatore Celzani…'

At the mention of Celzani, the engineer gave a little laugh. 'Ah, as for old Mr Celzani, you'd best leave him alone.'

'What?' asked Miss Pedani. 'Does he not attend all the exhibitions from beginning to end that are given at the gymnasium, schools and institutes? His approval means a great deal. You cannot deny Commendatore Celzani's seriousness.'

'I certainly don't deny it – far from it!' Ginoni replied energetically. 'All the more because he is my good friend. On the contrary, I say that he is one of the most venerable greybeards in Turin. But…' and here he cast a furtive glance at the children while scratching his chin, as if he were looking for a way to make sense without being understood by them. But the children were busy dividing up the sweets and were not paying any attention to him.

'But,' he began again, 'his worship of gymnastics is too one-sided. Is he fascinated just as enthusiastically with boys' gymnastics? And then, has he expressed an interest in older girls rather than younger ones? However, his diligence in going to such exhibitions is admirable, as is the attention he gives them. The great enjoyment that he derives from gymnastics is, er… intellectual. He departs from them filled with seriousness, with his soft, blue eyes half-closed, lost in deepest contemplation. Ah, if one could only write it down. I know his type, and he is not the only one. Female gymnastics has been an incomparable discovery for these gentlemen, a true consolation of their old age, a source of the most delicious cerebral delights of which we ordinary people can have but a faint inkling. Old Celzani's interest has nothing to do with scientific gymnastics, you can take it from me. You'd best quote other authorities, Miss!'

'One day I'll quote *you*,' replied the teacher in order to cut short the discussion, 'because I'll persuade you, and have you enrol at the gymnasium.'

Everyone laughed.

'Never, whilst I still breathe!'[21] exclaimed the engineer in mock seriousness. 'Or if I do go to the gymnasium, it will only be to see you on the parallel bars.'

'And you will have a lot to look at,' the young lady answered. 'Did you know that there are five hundred movements on the parallel bars alone?'

The engineer was about to answer with a slightly inappropriate jest when the doorbell rang, and a moment later the secretary entered.

This caused a sensation.

He came to present his uncle's regrets since he could not leave the house because of a cold. He entered without thinking that the teacher would be there, and when he saw her it was as if he had felt a strong electrical jolt; just as startling was the great fear of being the object of stares. Still, he could not overcome the immediate and desperate need to find on her face some impression of his letter; so he stared at her, dilating his small eyes and making an exceedingly strange face while every muscle in his body trembled, and he began to blush a bright red, but this was soon replaced by a sickly pallor.

That face revealed everything to Mr Ginoni in a flash; he glanced quickly at the teacher, who allowed an indefinable smile to escape, though it was expressed by neither her mouth nor her eyes, but was somehow diffused on her immobile face; one might say that it was an outward reflex caused by a humorous image.

The secretary delivered his message, hardly moving his large lips, as if they had been stuck together with glue.

'My, my, my...' said the engineer to himself relishing his little discovery, as he brought the secretary the chair on which the new visitor sat as if on a pile of red-hot coals; the host then offered him a glass of Malvasia. The secretary took it and held it next to his chest in a priestly pose.

All at once Mr Ginoni conceived and set in action a plan of merciless teasing. 'So, my dear secretary,' he said, 'you have arrived in the middle of a discussion of gymnastics. We were speaking with the physical education teacher. We need to determine which school you belong to – is it the school of Baumann? Or perhaps that other school – which one is it, Miss Pedani? Oh yes, Obermann! Is it the school of Obermann? What are your ideas related to the effect of gymnastics on the functions of the heart?'

The teacher rolled her eyes toward the ceiling. The secretary was petrified and quickly raised the glass to his mouth and stared at the engineer. Then he swallowed the wine in one gulp and arose in confusion. 'My dear Mr Ginoni, you are joking. I regret that I cannot remain longer, but I must return immediately to my uncle.'

'Oh no, sir,' said Ginoni. 'I cannot allow you to leave like that. In addition, you cannot leave now because the front door to the building remains open until eleven, and you never know whom you might meet on the stairway. Naturally, because you are a chivalrous person, it is both an act of courtesy as well as your duty to accompany Miss Pedani to her door.'

The secretary immediately sat down again, but young Ginoni scowled because he had hoped to be the one to accompany the lady.

'I am not afraid of anybody,' the teacher said with virile determination.

'It is not enough not to be afraid,' replied Ginoni. 'You must also inspire fear in others, and you do not have that talent.'

Young Ginoni then steered the conversation elsewhere, questioning Miss Pedani on the great festivals that had been announced for the Gymnastics Congress of Frankfurt, and this gave him the opportunity to even the score. They would surely be the most beautiful festivals that had ever been celebrated in Germany. Participants from all over Europe had been invited, among whom were many from Italy. He envied her fortunate colleagues who would see a spectacle that was unique in the world and who would make the acquaintance of the most illustrious gymnasiarchs of the German States such as Kloss, Niggeler, Danneberg, the famous father of gymnastics Turnvater Jahn, and many others – while she, unfortunately, could not even obtain their portraits.[22]

While the young man spoke, the secretary shot sidelong glances at Miss Pedani, deeply jealous of the apparent familiarity with which she communicated with the young man, and at the same time disconsolate to see all her thoughts and feelings turned to gymnastics with so much ardour that it left little hope that she could comprehend any other passion in her heart. Despite this, a little glint of hope sparkled in his eye, and at that moment he became anxious and impatient to leave and to go with her.

Celzani jumped out of the chair when he saw Miss Pedani get up and prepare to leave.

But the engineer was merciless. 'Now that I think of it,' he said as they all arose, 'the secretary is so timid with the ladies that he might just leave the teacher at the second floor, so I'd better go with her, too.'

Great God! For Celzani those words were like the slap of an icy hand across his face, but he did not dare to remonstrate. And while everyone said their goodbyes and the student shook the teacher's hand, Celzani observed a fleeting expression on her face as if he had squeezed her hand too tightly, and this amounted to a second slap in the face for the poor man. All three of them left and slowly climbed the partially darkened stairway. The engineer continued to chatter wittily, but owing to his great pain the secretary could not find a single word to say. Celzani proceeded up weakly, stopping when Ginoni and the teacher stopped and lagging behind a little every now and then in order to gaze lovingly at the beautiful woman; it was as if he were either trying to extract a response from her figure or looking daggers at his jailer's back. When they were in front of the door, where the light of the gas lamp did not reach, the engineer struck a match and the teacher rang the bell. The secretary was ready to view and interpret the parting glance, and in fact, as she went in, she looked at him, but alas, the look said nothing. And at the exact moment that the match went out, so too was extinguished all his hope.

The engineer guessed that his silence resulted from the sadness of disappointment and, emboldened by the darkness, he said to him point blank, 'My dear secretary, you are in love with the teacher.'

The secretary jolted upright, denied everything, became enraged, and appeared amazed and offended at the joke.

'Why ever not?' Ginoni asked half seriously, half facetiously. 'Is it some sort of a disgrace, then? She is a beautiful and honest girl, not to mention highly original – out of the ordinary. Why don't you tell me the truth? I am her good friend, and I can give her some good advice. I am a gentleman, and I respect such feelings.'

Mr Celzani stood silently in the dark for a little while; then he replied with a voice choked with emotion, 'Well then, it is true.'

'It's about time,' said the engineer. 'There is nothing better than sincerity. Meanwhile you have experienced a disappointment – it is to be understood – but do not be discouraged. I know women, and I know the character of the teacher. She is one of those bombs that have a long and hidden fuse that burns secretly for a while, but then bursts into a tremendous explosion when one least expects it. Brace yourself with iron persistence and have the patience of a saint, and one day... I assume that you are pursuing her for the right reasons, *n'est-ce pas?*'

'Sir, you amaze me!' replied Celzani. 'My intentions are honourable!'

'But that is what I want to talk about,' the engineer said (assuming a facetious tone because of that little misunderstanding). 'Well then, listen to a little advice. Women like that cannot be taken by a direct assault; you need to use strategy. She has a passion: gymnastics. Well, arrange to seize her by the handle of that passion. You need to become a member of the gymnasium, exercise, study the subject in books, speak about it to her and by those means enter into her good graces. This is the first advice that I will give you; afterwards there will be much more. But now, to the gymnasium! Courage.'

Uncertain whether Ginoni was speaking sincerely or from jest, Celzani did not answer. Meanwhile, they had reached the Commendatore's door.

'Good night,' said the engineer. 'I am a gentleman, and I will keep your secret.'

The secretary answered him with a weak and mistrustful, 'Good night,' and he re-entered the house, heartily sorry that he had said anything at all.

Despite his shame and discouragement, when he entered the room a hope still flashed before him as he lit the candle on the bedside table. Who knows? Perhaps she had written him that very day, and the letter would arrive the next morning. Unfortunately, he could easily guess the contents of that letter, but whatever might transpire, it would seem to him less cruel than that mute indifference that crushed him down. With that thought, he undressed and craned his ear, since his room was directly beneath Miss Pedani's and the floor was thin, so he could hear even the smallest noise. But presently he heard nothing; she must have been at the little reading table. Just then a suspicion came to him and with it a new hope: he had perhaps done a bad thing in not expressing clearly in his declaration his intentions for marriage. She had perhaps believed that he had merely asked for an exchange of affection. What an awful mistake he had made! And yet the letter had seemed so clear!

Great God, how beautiful she was! He had never seen her looking so well as she had that evening, sitting there with an

43

erect torso like an empress on a throne with that ample bosom quivering with life – a bosom on which he would gladly have lolled his head even if it meant he would be grilled alive. The light from the large lamp gave to her complexion such a youthful glow that it made one think that she must have grown younger by a year for each kiss that was given to her. He had observed her hand, which was a bit thickened by gymnastic exercise, resting on the table; still it was long and beautiful, full of strength and elegance, and he had wanted to swoop down upon it like a vulture on a turtledove. Ah no, surely she was not attracted to him; her ideal must be a completely different sort of man! And yet he felt inside him the flood of passion that fills all the voids, that equalises all the differences and that challenges every comparison. His brain swirled around like a wheeling windmill.

At the first noise that he heard from above, he bolted upright in the bed and stared with reddened eyes and bated breath at the ceiling. Never had the noises so agitated him as they had that night. He knew them all, and by means of them he followed all of her movements: moving the chair, wandering around the room throwing her clothes here and there, opening and closing the armoire, putting the candlestick on the little night table, dropping one boot, then another…

Oh, how cruel life was! It was just at that moment that poor Celzani felt most forcefully his resentment of Nature, which seemed to have created him precisely for an ecclesiastical career. He would have given twenty years of his life if he could have changed his face. But then, little by little, as his vigil dragged on and as his desires were frustrated, he grew tired. Still, he was comforted by feelings of warm and humble sadness, during which he left off contemplating the object of his adoration and contented himself with imagining her things, which he had heard her drop one by one, and it seemed that it would have been enough for him to have those items: to caress them, to kiss them, to bite them gently as an outlet for his feelings.

He hardly slept that night, and he awakened before dawn in order to await the familiar sounds that would begin again all the violence of desire that had been calmed by his fatigue. And in fact, at the precise hour when Miss Pedani was accustomed to arise, he heard the thud of bare feet on the floor, and that shook everything. He heard the usual rustle that she made when she dressed, then the dull sound of the dumb-bells that were pulled out from under the bed because every day as soon as she had arisen she did a few exercises. And that final image of those strong young arms waving about over her head gave him the impetus to do something dramatic. He wanted to shorten the suffering of uncertainty, so he would wait for her at the door at half past eight and demand an answer from her.

He indeed waited for her, and by a stroke of good luck, she descended alone. He approached her, greeted her and asked with a trembling voice, 'Do you have anything to tell me?'

The teacher answered calmly, 'Yes. Only one thing. I must thank you for your kind thoughts.'

'Nothing more?'

'No, Secretary,' she replied politely, 'nothing more.'

And she left.

Thus began a series of extremely melancholy days for him; despite this, he had decided to enter the fray again with a formal proposal of marriage, but he understood that to do so at once after his recent humiliation and without preparing the ground would have been folly. In the meantime, one misfortune after another rained down upon him.

The first of these was that Miss Zibelli suddenly stopped speaking to him. He would have been less affected by this had he known that she had entered into one of her phases brought on by disappointment in the world. She exhibited this dissatisfaction by walling herself inside a kind of forced enthusiasm for her vocation as a teacher. This showed itself when she began reading her schoolbooks even in the street; blinding herself to youth and love, which passed her on all sides; becoming pedantically zealous of her duties; being stern with her pupils, their families, her colleagues – with the whole world. But Rev. Celzani knew nothing of this; he was ignorant of the true cause of her discourtesy. He was good and kind with everyone, and he could only see her sudden impulse of antipathy, which wounded him deeply.

Next, he found the behaviour of the teacher Fassi to be odd. The teacher encountered Celzani in the stairway and showed him the proofs of an article entitled 'Berlin spends half a million per year on gymnastics', in which a comparison was made with Italy, which spent only half as much for the entire country; and then he abruptly switched the subject to Miss Pedani. 'What a big, beautiful girl she is!' he exclaimed. 'She would be worthy of marrying the handsomest man in Italy. I suspect that you are incapable of lifting overhead with both hands the two dumb-bells that she lifts with only one hand. Whoever marries her will first have to take this into account.'

What kind of talk was this? Celzani did not feel offended by the comparisons of their strength; his one thought was of their disparity of beauty. As for the rest, he had a clear conscience – but the thing that worried him was his suspicion that the teacher had guessed his intentions.

A few days later Fassi returned to the same subject. 'I have just been upstairs with Miss Pedani, and she is trying out a new combination for girls with the heavy wand. She is always trying new exercises, and she does not have time for any amorous distractions. It's also perhaps because she has not found anyone to suit her. As you know, even in love – I will say it thus since you understand Latin – "*similia cum similibus*",[23] and where would she find a man who is equal to her? She despises weaklings, and if she were to be foolish enough to shackle herself to one of those… well, woe to him!' And he stared at the secretary, but once again he stirred up a great fear that the teacher had read his thoughts rather than merely the words that he spoke; but rather than dampening his desires, this knowledge stirred up his feelings, and he later recalled them with emotions that were practically sensual in nature.

There was worse to come, however. Two or three times as he and Miss Pedani walked down the stairs, he saw young Ginoni come out on the landing wearing an aggressive expression on his face; and every time after seeing the secretary, the young man made an angry gesture and went back in the house. One morning Celzani saw the young man follow the teacher at a considerable distance as she walked down the via San Francesco d'Assisi, and this caused him great pain. The youth, charm and impudence of that blond-headed nit filled him with horror, so he decided to keep an eye on him every day.

But the most serious trouble came from Mr Fassi's wife. She watched out for him for a few days, and she finally caught him one day in front of the main door. 'How is Mr Fassi?' Celzani asked. With her whiny voice that sounded as if it had been emitted from a tightly laced mid-section, she replied (as was her wont) by glorifying her husband's great work. 'He is upstairs working on a comparison between the salaries of gymnastics teachers in Sweden and Italy. Because it is a scandal that must end: to speak of the years of study that it requires, and then gymnastics teachers are paid the same as bank clerks who don't even have the honour of being a professor; all they are taught to do is scribble away furiously. When I think about it, with his talent and his personality, what a career he could have had! You have no idea the amount of work that man does. He is constantly disturbed in every sort of way by duties, by visits. That teacher Miss Pedani is there all the time to ask for help or advice. I ask you, should a young woman hang about a man in the prime of his life? Is that an indecent liberty? And remember, I am there the whole time; can you imagine if I were not there? After that, judge the girl by the impression that she makes; she should be the very picture of dignity. Really! This young lady who has been attending school for years actually stood up in her anatomy class last year and without realising her ignorance asked the teacher, "Sir, where is the sympathetic nerve?" Well, that says it all!'[24]

Seeing with a quick glance the effect that she produced in Mr Celzani, she forged on ahead with the appearance of saying things that did not concern him. 'Anyway, I could really say a lot more. These young teachers who have worked in half a dozen towns before coming to Turin… well, we've all heard about the adventures of teachers in little villages. There is one such story about a company of artillerymen that has been making the rounds.[25] What surprises me is that she was ever hired in Turin. The only thing for sure is that she is well known in town and that she has quite a reputation. Enough said, though; my own opinion is that we will learn some interesting things before much more time has passed.'

After this she told several other nasty stories about the neighbours, but the secretary heard nothing more, and although he distrusted her words, he remained stunned after she had departed. The idea that the girl might have had an ugly past gave him feelings of inexpressible bitterness, intense jealousy and heart-rending torment. In particular, that artillery company pursued him and bayoneted him in the ribs for a week afterwards. He suffered even more because for several days he was not able to see her, and although he was anxious to know and to free himself from that horrible doubt, he knew neither whom to turn to nor what he could do. Finally, one morning he encountered her, and the greater part of his suspicions evaporated as soon as he saw her. No, Great God, it was not possible: everything about her from her head to her toes repudiated the calumny; her beautiful body glowed all over with the haughtiness of a vigorous virginity, issuing intact and triumphant from every battle as if it were enchanted armour. But an hour later his suspicions revived, and his previous worries returned stronger than ever.

But something happened at that time that impelled him to a sudden resolution. He encountered the teacher Mr Fassi one morning, who said out of the blue and as a continuation of their previous conversation, 'Oh, that Pedani. What a Spartan! I got a look at her from my lavatory: she had some poor soul with her who had gone there to learn calisthenics, and Pedani keeps plenty of windows wide open despite the freezing temperatures! She is a firm believer in the need for fresh air when doing gymnastics.'

The secretary did some rapid calculations to himself: if the teacher could see Pedani's room from his bathroom, then how much better must the view be from the dormer window of the attic that was located directly above Fassi's lavatory. As soon as he was alone, he hurriedly went back in the house, took the key to the attic, bolted in long strides up the stairs, opened the door and proceeded hunched over to avoid the low beams of the roof. In the middle of the attic were pieces of lumber, broken furniture and heaps of tiles. He approached the dormer, climbed up on a bundle of sticks, stretched out as far as he could and stuck his face out into the void. He then made an exclamation of pleasure. The window of the room located on the opposite wall of the house was wide open; Miss Pedani was standing sideways toward the window, turned to face her pupil who was not visible. Her sonorous contralto voice reached to the roof very clearly.

'But no,' she said, 'this is not the way to make a "simple, jumping half-step" for me. You're doing a "long, jumping step". You have not understood. Do it again.'

The secretary heard the step of the invisible pupil.

'No,' repeated the instructor, 'it's still too exaggerated.'

Oh, that beautiful, deep, warm, resonant voice, which would have made him imagine an admirable body even if he had closed his eyes!

Miss Pedani seemed dissatisfied with the second attempt also because she shook her head vigorously and eagerly lifted up her black skirt with both hands in order to reveal the movement of her feet. 'Pay attention!' she said, 'and do like this.'

'Great God!' moaned the secretary. He saw a flash of whiteness that flickered above her boots and which blinded him as if it were a ray of sunlight beamed into his eyes from a mirror, and the blood rushed to his face as if he had been turned upside down. It was only a moment, but it was enough. He did not hear any other commands; he jumped down from the pile of sticks, brushed off the dried leaves and twigs with trembling hands, and with that vision of whiteness still in his eyes he practically ran across the attic once more. He descended the stairs with resolute steps, and after re-entering the house, he sat down at his desk, placed his head in his hands and collected his thoughts. He had decided once and for all to go all the way with an open and explicit offer of marriage.

But Celzani had a duty that he felt he could not dismiss: he had to speak first with his uncle and to ask for his approval and his advice; there was another reason: if the proposal were done with the old man's consent, and perhaps by him in person, it would have even greater chances of success. Passion had blinded him to the point that he did not doubt for a second that the old man would agree. At worst, he would probably not give him a definite 'no'; he would hesitate, he would consider the issue, in short, he would give him hope that he would not have the heart to take away. He therefore prepared his speech, and when he had the first sentence and the general gist well in mind, he entered the Commendatore's room with a serious expression and with his hands clasped on his chest. He seated himself in front of his uncle and asked permission to speak; then slowly, with trembling voice and downcast eyes, he revealed his secret.

The Commendatore was a man who was surprised by nothing because he gave very little importance to the things of this world, but when he heard what was being discussed, he could do little more than raise his stately white head upright from the back of the chair and look into his nephew's eyes. Letting his head sink back again, and wrapping himself more tightly in his dressing gown, he listened to the rest of the story as his eyes wandered listlessly over the ceiling frescoes. The secretary had had the good luck to encounter the man while he was in an extremely good mood because he was to go that very day with a school inspector from Milan to see a demonstration of female gymnastics at the Soccorso Institute.[26] On the other hand, when he was forced away from the delights of his little fantasy world, he was almost always impatient to re-enter it every time he was obliged to leave, so he would never contradict anyone, and by refusing to do anything or by doing just the opposite of what others expected him to, he could avoid granting either a consent or a promise.

When his nephew had finished, old Celzani looked first at his immaculate fingernails and then at his embroidered slippers, and murmured a vague word or two that was not an outright approval, but neither was it a disapproval. He meant to say only that one should proceed with caution. Without a doubt, the girl was admirable and had the looks and behaviour of a person worthy of respect, but (and this was the upshot of his statement) before proceeding further, he believed that it was expedient to look deeper into the matter. And while his nephew looked at him with a puzzled and uneasy expression, the old man hemmed, hawed and looked around, and then he blurted out the suggestion that his nephew should consult his friend the Cavaliere Pruzzi, superintendent of the city schools, who most certainly should be able to give accurate and minute details regarding any aspect of the teaching personnel. This advice seemed excellent to Rev. Celzani. The old man counted out the days on his fingers, and settled on next Saturday as the most opportune day; he need only present one of his visiting cards. No matter what the outcome of the business might be, the Cavaliere Pruzzi was a man one could count on to keep a secret with the most scrupulous delicacy. He said this as if it were something of merely secondary importance, and then turned to another subject.

The great happiness that Rev. Celzani received from that half approval was deeply marred in the following days by the reawakening of the sad suspicions that had been planted in his heart by Mrs Fassi. These quickly magnified and had such a terrible effect on his imagination that on the appointed day he ascended the interminable stairs of the city hall as if he were an invalid going to the doctor to hear a sentence of death. Despite the fact that he knew that the Cavaliere Pruzzi was an excellent man and that they were acquainted, he was repelled by having to confess his passion and his intentions, since he would not be able to turn to the delicate questions that were necessary without a confession.

He timidly entered the modest office of the superintendent. It was a small room illuminated by a single window and surrounded by shelves on which one could see written in large letters the names of all the schools in Turin. The superintendent was bent over a pile of papers with his elbows on the desk, absent-mindedly fingering his wig. When Celzani saw him, so little and fat with that kind, flaccid, beardless face on which one could constantly read worried thoughts of his 'enormous responsibilities', he recovered some of his confidence.

The superintendent received him with a face full of laugh lines as if it were a cracked terracotta mask. He gave the young man a seat in front of him, took the visiting card from his uncle and invited him to speak. The secretary was a bit surprised when after he had expressed with difficulty and confusion the purpose of his visit, he could detect not the slightest sign of wonderment. His listener merely nodded his head and assumed an expression of seriousness, as if to say, 'Sir, right now I am a public official.'

When Celzani had finished, Mr Pruzzi fingered the forelock of his wig and said gravely, 'This is a delicate matter.' Then he asked for the teacher's first and last names and what section she belonged to.

When he had heard everything, he put his two hands on his eyes and remained absorbed in thought like this, as if he were looking for the physical and moral characteristics of the young lady in the midst of that small female army whose many faces he retained in his extremely acute memory.

'Good lord!' he exclaimed suddenly, remembering the face, and surprised not to have recalled sooner a figure that was so original. He gave the secretary a long, slow look as if to compare his figure with hers. Then he slowly scratched the end of his nose with the tip of his index finger. Bending his head a little, he said, 'I am happy for you.' But it was too late; Rev. Celzani had understood the results of the comparison. He did not take offence at this but waited anxiously.

'So,' the superintendent began to say with shortness of breath as he took out of the desk a sheet of paper which he began to fold and refold without looking at the secretary, 'you would like some information – which is natural – of a personal nature, as has been said. But it is not so easy as you might suppose to give it to you. Just think of it, with five hundred teachers – how can one know them all? I'm buried under a mountain of responsibilities, worries and troubles. It's true: we have had a most unfortunate winter; a plethora of absences in all sections. It might be said that all the married teachers have agreed to increase the population this month. Then there are those blasted families where both are teachers! When the wife is sick the husband has to be absent; when her husband is ill the wife stays home; when the baby is sick, they both miss work. We won't even speak of the young ladies who encounter a little draught and then catch a cold. And then there are the troubles caused by the "monthly curse". Look here at the Savoy district which shows the number of absences – it's a virtual hospital![27] What can be done? Keep sending a doctor from the city to ascertain the situation at home? Good heavens! Besides, it isn't always convenient. There should be a fine for every unauthorised absence. But how could we do that? Oh, certainly there are some special cases where one should follow one's heart… yes, certainly. I assure you, my dear Celzani, this is a serious issue, very serious indeed.' And here he breathed a great sigh as if he were trying to catch his breath after a race, and the secretary made a respectful gesture to recall the superintendent back to the original subject.

'Ah!' he said, 'You are here for information. Rightly so, as I said. You might well imagine what it is like to oversee hundreds of young ladies, the greater part of whom are young, many – indeed, too many – are pretty, lively and extremely independent, who are dispersed over a large city and in the suburbs to a distance of two or three miles from the centre of town. Naturally, one does what one can, since we want proper decorum, but in short, we cannot have a squad of policemen to supervise the teachers' gentleman callers. And we certainly cannot overstep the bounds of what we feel is "reasonable freedom". No, it is an extremely delicate matter. And you cannot imagine the accusations, the concealed vengeance, the intrigues; we receive piles of anonymous letters…' And here he lost his breath for a moment.

'There are certain persons who cause us to despair because – through no fault of their own – Mother Nature has made them in such a way that they attract the eyes of others. I will not even mention the endless complaints that flood in from the families because of an unfair grade, an unwarranted disciplinary action, a classroom that is either too cold or too hot, a cough, the mumps or eye troubles. And then there are the female teachers who are offended by every word and believe that they are being persecuted; and lady principals – those blasted principals – who are like mother superiors from another era. And add a thicket of questions for every awards examination, every transfer, every preferment, every reprimand… Imagine the difficulty, my dear sir, imagine the delicacy, imagine the tact that is required.' And he made his point with a deep sigh.

'Sir, if you please,' said the secretary timidly, 'the information.'

'I'm coming to the information,' replied the superintendent. 'Naturally, it would be a great deal easier to give information about a male teacher. In such a case one would only have to ask, "Is he a gentleman or not, a monarchist or a republican, does he have debts or not, does he drink or not?" I know all of this by heart; you need only ask me. But what about the female teachers? What can I do? It is a complex thing; it is a thorny issue. Besides, knowing what I do, I must tread very carefully. They have fathers, brothers, relatives. You think that you have taken the right disciplinary steps, and two days later you find yourself in a dead-end street face-to-face with a strange man with a bushy beard who stares you in the face with two beady eyes while threatening you with a club. One can get into some real trouble. You mustn't forget either that they often run to the newspapers for no real reason. And for me the newspapers are, you see… well, the newspapers are a calamity in situations like this; they can do such evil. I will tell you frankly, the newspapers frighten me. I am frightened not for myself, but for the administration and for the issue of discipline. It is for these reasons that I am frightened. Do you not see what this office is like, my dear sir, do you not see the responsibility that I have on my shoulders, do you not see the sort of accountability that I owe to the public and to my conscience?' Gasping as he said this, he rested his neck for a moment on the back of the chair.

A dark suspicion then passed over the secretary's mind that the superintendent did not want to speak because it would cause him to tell some grave secrets – things that he could neither excuse nor explain. The secretary rose to his feet in order to force the superintendent to give him the *coup de grâce* while he was standing. 'In short,' he said with an emotion-choked yet resolute voice, 'tell me if you know something, whatever it might be. What information can you give me about Miss Pedani? I ask about her frankly and precisely, also in the name of my uncle.'

'But,' replied the superintendent, 'I know nothing. She is an excellent teacher. This I can absolutely verify. As for the rest…' Celzani bent forward in a sort of human question mark, 'There is nothing to say,' added the superintendent, 'that I know of. There might be… but there is not. Allow me to explain: one could say the same thing about every beautiful girl – that she has admirers; they might be suitors. I'm sure that you understand me.'

Mr Celzani asked him if he knew of anything concrete. Had she ever given cause for censure in her private life? Was there nothing in the official record regarding her conduct in the rural communities where she had been?

'But if I tell you that I do not know, that there exist no records,' Superintendent Puzzi replied, 'because of my friendship for your uncle, if anything could be ascertained relating to this case of a serious nature, I would tell you. But there is nothing… or rather…'

'Or rather?' asked the secretary.

'Or rather,' continued the superintendent, 'I would tell you, if I permitted myself to advise a friend, the negative information in the official records in such cases contains little; it is better to search by other means: look into the family. She is from Lombardy – from Brescia if I am not mistaken. But proceed with caution, one can never be too careful. Except…'

'Except what?' repeated Celzani.

'Except,' said the superintendent with a gesture that was quite emphatic, 'if I were to speak honestly, I would ask you what you really want. A teacher – all teachers in my opinion – should be required to be only teachers. They have a mission in life; we should leave them to dedicate their lives to it like nuns. Let everyone find his own way. And then, one never knows for sure. Pardon me if I express my real thoughts to you freely, but this is outside of the subject at hand. I repeat, nothing has been recorded. However, I say again: find out from other sources and proceed with care. I advise you because of the good will that I have for the Celzani family. And now, I have nothing further to say.'

A new suspicion suddenly occurred to Rev. Celzani. Was this a secret manoeuvre on the part of his uncle to extricate himself from the annoyance of an outright refusal or the bother of persuading him to go slowly; had the old man induced the superintendent to keep him on tenterhooks with his vague words? He tried nevertheless one final test. 'You are aware of my situation,' he said. 'You can imagine the state of my heart. Will you give me your word of honour that you have told me everything that you know?'

At that moment a clerk entered with a parcel of letters and the mail. 'But what's the point of giving you my word?' replied the superintendent with a deep sigh of exasperation. 'With this stack of things to do as you can see, I don't have a minute to breathe and I don't know where to start. Good heavens! Everything that I could say, I have attempted to tell you, and you know that I have great affection for your uncle. And so then, good day. And follow my advice.' Then, as if to compensate him, he added softly, 'A beautiful girl, however.' Then he pushed him politely into the hallway.

In conclusion, poor Celzani was left with new doubts as well as former fears, and he returned home so dissatisfied, afflicted and anxious that he did not even take the time to report on the visit to his uncle. And the fact that the old man did not ask him about it that same evening confirmed the secretary's suspicions that his relative had worked behind the scenes to his detriment. Because of this, he remained hurt and resentful. But that divine whiteness that he had seen from the dormer window glowed eternally in front of his eyes like a warm fire of electric light, and in spite of everything and everyone, that vision caused his love to blaze up ever more stubbornly and fervently.

Even so, with the superintendent's vacuous information, Celzani understood clearly that his uncle had even more of a logical pretext to deny him the consent that he needed. He had to accept this, although he had not relinquished all suspicions that he was the victim of a plot. But since he was at his wits' end, he conceived the risky idea of confiding in Mr Ginoni; he sought him out and stated his case and asked for his advice. The engineer was surprised at him. What need was there for information? It's not the sort of thing that everyone needs to know – but do you want more? For his part, he could vouch for her; after all, he knew a few things. She was from Brescia, an orphan, the daughter of an army doctor who had died many years previously; she had a brother, an honest merchant who lived in New Grenada.[28]

This news pleased Mr Celzani. What other information did he want to ask? Ginoni continued, 'Do you want to send a circular to all the mayors of the towns where she was a teacher? It's absurd. A girl is always a mystery; the only thing you can do is to trust her face and the feelings of your own heart. Better still, my dear secretary, tell me this: at what point should we determine how she feels about you?'

Rev. Celzani's face clouded over with discouragement, and he lowered his eyes much like a priest in front of the altar; the engineer couldn't help but chuckle, but at the same time he pitied the poor man. 'Listen,' he said, 'what if I were to put in a little word in your favour… Eh? What would you say to that? Could anyone give a better proof of friendship? If I were to delve into her heart a bit…'

'Delve away,' the secretary answered sadly.

'We will delve, then,' said the engineer. 'One never knows. Who sees more clearly into a girl's heart than a disinterested examiner? Let me do this, and you can go about your business and be happy.'

Indeed, Ginoni proposed to do what he had promised, not only because the oddity of the psychological case involving these two singular people interested him, but also because he had suspected for several days that his son (whose motivations he knew very well) had been meeting the teacher on the stairway; so far she had abstained from complaining to him so as to spare the engineer any unpleasantness. It seemed to him to be good paternal politics to put an impediment between his son and Pedani.

Upon leaving the following morning, he found Miss Pedani on the landing; she was standing with his own maid, to whom she was suggesting certain gymnastic exercises to cure the chilblains. Baumann had been the first to discover that gymnastics on school benches could prevent this malady.[29] Miss Pedani explained the process to her thoroughly.

At the sight of her employer, the maid went back in, and Ginoni made his usual jocular greeting to the teacher, 'Down with gymnastics!'

The young lady replied energetically in the same vein, 'Down with those who cause lymphangitis and rickets!' The engineer laughed, and he proceeded to walk with her down the staircase, then abruptly he asked in a low voice, 'However can you be so calm while there are wretches who suffer a thousand deaths because of you?'

She stared at him and asked, 'Who has told you this?'

'The one who wrote to you.'

'In that case,' the teacher said with indifference, 'let us talk about something else.'

'What? You won't even talk about it?' the engineer asked. 'Have you no sense of pity? Is this how gymnastics hardens the heart?'

'No,' she replied. 'I do not have a hard heart, but it is already occupied.' She explained that she was dominated by one sole passion, and she had decided to dedicate her entire youth to it. In any case, she would not link her life to any other man but one who wished to dedicate his own life to the same field. And she said matter-of-factly, 'Whoever marries me will be a great gymnast.'

The engineer chuckled under his moustache, and then turning to look at her, he said, 'I believe you.' Then he asked, 'So the fate of the poor unfortunate has been irrevocably decided?'

'No one's fate depends on me,' she replied. 'But enough of this.'

'Amen!' murmured Ginoni.

They descended the last flight of stairs in silence.

'And yet,' said the engineer in the main doorway, 'are you still thinking about it?'

'Certainly not,' replied Miss Pedani, 'I was thinking about something completely different. I was thinking to myself that we do not allow nearly enough exercises for little girls' lower limbs. Look to yourself!'

The engineer gave a laugh, and as he left her, he exclaimed, 'Down with Sparta!'

And turning back, Pedani shouted, 'Down with Sybaris!' and then she marched away with energetic strides down the sidewalk.[30]

Rev. Celzani was cut to the quick by the answer, even though it had been sweetened a bit by the engineer who had reported it to him, and he was not comforted a bit by Ginoni's exhortations that he should not give up. The engineer repeated the metaphor of the bomb with the long fuse that would undoubtedly explode later. The secretary then returned to his former tormented and suffering state. He continued to spy on the teacher when she went out or came back in and to meet or follow her, but this time his desperation gave him greater courage. Each time he gazed at her it was with long inquiring and importuning looks as he tipped his hat like a beggar who asked only for a smile and a bit of pity. She was always the same with him, greeting him with courtesy and indifference and without ostentation, pretending not to notice that he waited for her behind the door, behind the pillars, in the corners, in the hallway and that he stood still for a moment after she passed in order to contemplate her. She understood in addition that the poor man's passion was growing more intense with each passing day. But unknown to her, there was a new reason for this.

Maria Pedani's reputation was growing. One of her articles on Per Henrik Ling – the founder of Swedish gymnastics – that was published in *The New Arena* was interesting because of its subject and for a certain plain and brusque vivacity of style, particularly in the description of the exercises on the 'window ladder' and the 'wall bars'.[31] This article was reproduced in a Turinese political newspaper and had made a considerable splash. One evening she gave a lecture at the Philotechnical Institute on the establishment of specialised curative gymnastics for certain deformities in children, and she displayed on that occasion an exceedingly rare understanding of anatomy that was not accompanied by any pedantic pretensions. The newspapers reported the event, discussing in glowing phrases her appearance, her odd but lovely voice and her singular methods of delivery using vigorous gestures, and all of these things combined to earn hearty applause for her. All of this made her much sought after for private lessons: there were aspiring teachers who came to the house to take gymnastics lessons since such courses were not offered at the gymnasium in those months; there were young girls who had deformities and did not want to exercise with others, and teachers who were already certificated who sought her expertise and assistance. Rev. Celzani frequently encountered them on the stairway and heard that name repeated with admiration by them and others inside and outside of the house.

Presently, this burgeoning fame gave a new outlet for his love, a piercing and delicious new stimulus to his desires. He felt a more refined voluptuousness when he imagined himself the certain possessor of a well-known and admired woman, he thought that he would be twice as happy in his own obscurity to have her after she returned from a well-received lecture, to take possession of that form that so many others had desired and caressed with their eyes. It rather seemed to him that his happiness would be so much sweeter and deeper precisely because he was small and unimportant next to her, nothing more than a husband, forgotten at certain times (even for most of the day); kept like a servant, a tool, a plaything, an overgrown house pet. Oh, great God! This inflamed his heart even more: that with his big melon of a head typical of a meditative man, he was not devoid of a certain priestly finesse, and he had read deeply into her nature, and he understood that when she had tied the knot, she was a woman who would remain rigidly faithful to her husband. It was only through feelings of proper dignity and the strength of his reason that he had so far kept himself in check. If he could only attain his goal! How little he would worry about the mockeries and deceptions of others then! He would be confident of his actions; he would know how to guard his treasure well right under the nose of the whole world. Let them laugh at Mr Fassi's little satires!

Certainly, Fassi continued to make little quips every time Celzani met him, but with new bitterness against Miss Pedani; as this became clear, the secretary avoided him. In addition Fassi was busy with other things, and so the much-needed collaboration between him and Pedani was cut back more and more. At the same time she had brought down upon herself a storm of criticism because of some provocative articles in *The New Arena*. She attacked all the adversaries of gymnastics by saying that by exercising only their lower limbs, ballet dancers had athletic legs but scrawny chests; she had accused fencing teachers of bulking up the hips and the right shoulder, but at the expense of pleasing proportions for the rest of the body; she criticised piano teachers by claiming that they were the principal cause of a sedentary life for girls; and surgeons who oppose gymnastics because it discredits their instruments of torture; she had even provoked the apothecaries and druggists, writing that they slandered the 'new science' because they had caused a reduction in the sale of codfish oil. From all sides came bitter replies, and Fassi found that he alone was left with the embarrassment of answering them and that Miss Pedani had virtually abandoned him in this situation. Mr Fassi revealed his frustration to the secretary, but naturally he did not give the real reason because although he considered her ambitious and ungrateful, still for his own interests he pretended to have the warmest relationship with her, but when the secretary defended her, Fassi grew more heated. One day they finally exchanged some sharp words. The teacher was provoked into saying some things that were more unpleasant than usual, and Mr Celzani responded resentfully, 'Miss Pedani is a good girl.'

'Pooh!' said Fassi, 'I wish that were so!'

'Oh! That's not true!' exclaimed Mr Celzani indignantly.

Fassi was ready to let fly with a big insult, but the thought of his reduced rent caused him to hold his tongue. Instead, he contented himself with saying, 'I only wish that she would not do her experimenting at my expense.'

The secretary made a retort, and they separated in a bad humour. From then on they only greeted one another with icy politeness.

But that dispute inflamed his love even more intensely. They were all conspiring to slander her and to oppose him: his uncle, Mr Fassi, Fassi's wife, the superintendent, Miss Zibelli; they were all liars. And yet he loved her more than ever; in fact he found in her severe, measured behaviour and in every mood or new movement additional proof of her perfection.

And then there was a new excitement: some masons who had been called in to repair the brickwork on the stairway had stretched a board across the place where they were working as a sort of bridge for the tenants, but when he left the house at just the right time, it was very sensual for Celzani to see Miss Pedani walk across this plank and to see the wood bend under her footsteps; in an odd sort of way this gave him an indirect (but extremely pleasant) sensation of her bulk. One morning he was extremely lucky. The board had been thrown aside; he stepped outside the door in time to position himself in the place where the teacher was about to pass, and she performed a violent act that allowed him to see her strength. She did not take advantage of the plank; instead she jumped over the missing stair in one leap, but while jumping she brushed his lowered face with her clothing, producing the effect of a voluptuous lash; she acknowledged him with a smile that made him happy for many days afterwards. Was it real or an illusion? After that day he thought that he could see something new in her eyes: a glint of kindness that seemed to be the beginning of a permanent metamorphosis, and he started to scrutinise her face with unusual ardour, as an astronomer might study the face of the sun: now reassuring, now doubtful because the metamorphosis was so subtle. Did he dare press his suit? Was it too soon? But what other encouragement could he hope for?

Then the engineer Ginoni came to him with help; he had a bright idea. Meeting Celzani one evening in the via San Francesco, he said, 'My dear Secretary, if you are a gentleman, you must do something. There is in Berry's shop window a photograph of the Baron Maignolt, the famous velocipedist who won the Paris-to-Versailles race. Miss Pedani is a great admirer of the Baron. You should get the portrait and give it to her. What do you say? You'll see that it will make a big hit. But mind you, giving photos is not enough; you need to emulate those who are photographed. Jog from Turin to Moncalieri as *The People's Gazette* mentions: you'll get farther with that than with ten years of sighing.'

Mr Celzani neither agreed nor disagreed, but by that evening he had already bought the photograph and given it to the teachers' cleaning girl. He expected very little from this act. Nevertheless, the next morning he waited for Miss Pedani, expecting little more than to receive a cold thank-you. She came down with Miss Zibelli, who upon seeing him bolted ahead without a word of greeting. Miss Pedani stopped, and she said with unusual liveliness and the most beautiful smile that he had ever seen, 'Oh, Mr Secretary, how kind you have been! How could you guess what I wanted?'

Celzani was overjoyed. And the teacher continued happily as she passed by, 'I don't know how I can repay you. Let me know if I can do anything for you.'

Oh, what cruelty! But Celzani was in seventh heaven; he was both blessed and deceived, for he seemed to have taken a huge step forward, and he only awaited the right time to pop the question. Uncle or no uncle, information or no information, he could not wait any longer; he needed to propose formally as soon as possible while the iron was hot. His only problem was whether he should ask her in person or in writing – this alone kept him from acting. In the mean time he began to plan with intricate concern the formulas that he would use in either case. But while he was formulating, events were moving forwards.

Miss Zibelli had made peace with her friend several days earlier, and this had been occasioned by a new development in her life. She had encountered one day a young gymnastics teacher in the entryway of the house; he was blond, elegant and a former sergeant in the engineer corps. She had once heard him (with great enjoyment) speak at a meeting of the Teachers' Financial Aid Society. He was going up to see Mr Fassi, with whom he was friendly. He had bowed deeply to her, and then accompanied her up the stairs, speaking with a particular expression of respect and sympathy. Two days later they found themselves in Fassi's house; the master was out, but it was obvious to Mrs Fassi that the two knew one another so she did not introduce them. Since the young man was teacher to the youthful inmates at La Generala prison, their conversation acquired a rather sensitive flavour as he explained how bloody brawls, rebellions and other violent incidents were avoided in that place thanks to the instruction of gymnastics, which is used to channel natural exuberance and the arrogance of the strong; after victories in public sporting displays, the athletes become less likely to oppress those who are seen as weaker. And continuing the discussion, he asked for explanations and advice and listened to the replies with such lively and courteous attention that she could not help but be moved. From this, with all the usual promptness, the illusion of love – along with joy, cordiality and friendship – was reborn in her. She reconciled herself with Miss Pedani, and she stifled the envy that had begun to consume her because of her friend's gymnastic glories. She was once more pleasant at school, and she threw off the black cloak of pedagogy in which she had enfolded herself for some time; she began to read books of literature once again and even to write some verses on the sly. She thus neglected the administration of the house, although she normally assumed all those duties. It was this new disposition of mind that made it necessary for

Miss Pedani to bring the rent money to the secretary on the first day of the month, and it was for this reason that Miss Pedani performed her friend's duties. She was a little taken aback because the duties involved going to see Rev. Celzani, but Miss Zibelli (although she had always been bitter towards him) was no longer jealous. 'Go on!' she said lightheartedly after handing her the money in an envelope, 'You'll make him happy.'

Maria Pedani took down from the bookshelf the *Medical Gymnastics* by Schreber that she had promised to Professor Padalocchi and left. She rang the bell at the old man's door, and he greeted her warmly; after taking the book, he told her that he had felt some little improvement after having done the deep breathing exercises. The teacher then advised him to try arm rotations, giving him anatomical explanations for the specific action of the gymnastic exercises on the upper extremities and on the function of the thoracic organs.

While Miss Pedani was giving these instructions, the secretary was all alone in the house, sitting at his uncle's desk with pen in hand. He had been searching for some time for just the right words for his solemn question – either written or spoken, whichever it would be. The effort had given him serious difficulties from the start since it meant that he had to harmonise beautifully the declaration of impassioned love with the seriousness of a marriage proposal that would show that his plans had been preceded by much meditation and decisiveness derived from a clear conscience. It was also necessary to include (naturally, with great delicacy) an indication of his not inconsiderable financial condition and to dangle the hopes of a future inheritance from his uncle (although he had a multitude of little nephews in Genoa and Milan). He considered, wrote and then crossed out the words, never satisfied; he was also a bit perturbed by the thought that it was the first of the quarter, and since she was in charge of such things, Miss Zibelli would come to him to bring the rent: a visit that had been unpleasant ever since she began to give him the silent treatment. Even so, the first sentence was now decided and unchangeable. It began, 'Dearest Miss, I am about to take an important step in a man's life…' and he had just finished putting the first full stop onto the page when the doorbell rang. 'That will be Zibelli,' he said to himself with bitterness, and he assumed a haughty expression to greet her.

At that instant the old serving woman leaned into the doorway and said, 'Mr Secretary, it's Miss Pedani with the rent.'

Celzani jumped to his feet, his face aflame. He could only stammer out, 'Have her come in,' and he made a feeble gesture. Miss Pedani entered, and the servant closed the door.

The appearance of the teacher produced in him an odd effect, as if everything around him had suddenly changed. The light in the room changed, the furniture changed position, the shapes of things confused him, in his eyes everything was altered – rather like when a coward fights a duel. He scurried around here and there looking for a chair as he stammered, 'Come in, come in,' and he went to get the most distant seat, putting it close to the desk, a bit too close he thought, so he removed it and put it crosswise from him. He then turned towards his visitor and without looking directly at her, motioned for her to take a seat. He sat across from her and took the envelope in his hand, but he could think of nothing better to do in order to have the time to compose himself than to take and count the money with great attention, as if he suspected her of trying to defraud him.

Then, with trembling lips, he said, 'Everything is as it should be,' and he took out a sheet of official paper to write the receipt. But as he started to write, he trembled with a tempest in his head; he was consumed with indecision: was the moment right to pop the question or was the time inopportune and fraught with danger? He was so consumed with this problem that instead of writing the usual words on the sheet, he wrote, 'Dearest Miss, I am about to take an important step in a man's life…'

He realised his error and blushed, tore up the sheet, took out another and started to write again, but still with that same tempest in his head. His sight grew dim, his hand shook, his words refused to come and his forehead was bathed in sweat.

Calm and serious, the teacher regarded him. She laughed at nothing; she had no sense of humour. If one had observed her at this point, one would have seen nothing in her eyes but a slight expression of compassionate curiosity, as if she were staring at someone suffering from a mental aberration.

When Celzani finally succeeded in writing his signature, his resolution was already restored. He folded the sheet, but kept it in his hand in order to delay her; he stood up, and his face turned from red to pale white. Then he began, 'Miss!'

What was then going on in his brain? Perhaps an unexpected hiccup of courage, perhaps the sudden realisation that it might have been better to talk about something else first so that his declaration of love would not seem so abrupt and over-anxious. In the event, instead of saying what he had prepared, all of a sudden he switched tactics. Swallowing the saliva down his dry throat in a nervous gulp, he murmured humbly, 'Miss, if you need any repairs…'

This time the young lady smiled slightly. She answered no; everything was in order in her apartment, and she thanked him for his courtesy, and rising, she reached out in order to take the receipt.

The time had come; it was now or never. The secretary withdrew the sheet of paper and was resolved to say the words that he had prepared and which the confusion of the moment had prevented him from saying. Despite the danger, he threw himself forward with a courage born of desperation. 'Miss,' he said again.

Certain persons who are not shy but who speak under the sway of a strong emotion, especially when they express themselves in terms that are unfamiliar to them, adopt a style, tones and gestures that involuntarily divert them from the feelings that they want to express, so that even though these persons are sincere, plain and humble, their words come out sounding bombastic, tortured, preachy, ill chosen and false. It is as if someone else entirely were speaking in their place, without understanding the meaning of the words and almost trying to make them fail in their purpose. This is what happened to poor Rev. Celzani. His hand beat his chest, his voice rose excessively, his head wheeled around as if he were following the flight of butterflies as they circled about the teacher, and he twitched his large lips in a hundred strange ways as if he were numb from the cold.

'My dear Miss,' he intoned, 'I have something to tell you. If you please, I beg you to forgive me. I know that this is not the place, but there are certain feelings (when they are honest and holy affections) and certain times when an honest man must say everything and when you must forgive everything and simply let him speak. I have already explained myself to you. You understand my feelings. Never, never – even from the very first day – have I trifled with you. Never! I have always maintained the same thought. As God is my witness, I have never in my heart of hearts ever harboured anything but the purest intentions, the most sacred goal of lifelong love; even if I have not written it, I stand here to say it. My dear Miss, I ask for your hand in marriage. Perhaps it is not the fashion, but I speak to a beautiful soul. The fruit is ripe. Consider it. It is an honest gentleman who speaks, and one whose uncle has given his blessing. Trust in my heart. My life is no longer my own. I ask only for your hand. Only one word! Pronounce my sentence.'

After he gasped out this speech, Celzani stared desperately at the teacher's face with wide-open eyes and a terrified expression on his face.

During the first part of this declaration, the teacher had smiled, but she listened seriously at the last part. She wrinkled her forehead when he had finished and blushed slightly, but this quickly faded. Then fixing her gaze on a calendar that was hung on the wall, she spoke with a very natural sounding voice that made a curious contrast to the secretary's. Her voice was deep, almost a baritone, and she answered, 'Look, Mr Celzani, I don't know how to beat about the bush when it comes to saying things as they should be said... How should I say this? I will tell you frankly what I think. Please forgive me: I can only thank you for your good intentions. In fact, I feel honoured. But, if I had been interested, I would have shown it right after your letter because I understood what was implied in it. I say that I am honoured – sincerely honoured. But here is the thing: I truly have no calling for matrimony. For my occupation I need to be free; I have decided to be free. And then... I am twenty-seven years old; if I had had other inclinations I would have followed them sooner. So, in short, I don't know how to find the words. It pains me; I am grateful to you, but that's all. Kindly give me the receipt.'

When he heard these words, Celzani's wounded love screamed in agony, and caused him to revert to his natural speech patterns.

'Oh no, my dear Miss, no!' cried Celzani as he trembled. 'You say these things because you don't understand. I'm not like the others. Is that what you think? I love you truly; I have suffered for a long time, and I think of no one but you. What can I do? You say, "I want to be free," well, what does that matter to me? I will not be your master. Oh, you don't understand me; I will be your servant. I will not try to be anything else; I am nothing; I'll submit to your authority – I'll be madly happy to do so! You don't know the real me; you have driven me to distraction. I'll give you my heart's blood and my sacred soul… Good God! Don't say no! Have mercy on a man of good character!' As he said this he extended his arms and leaned forward in front of her, lifting up his face in supplication like Murillo's picture of *Saint Anthony before the Christ Child*.

The teacher was amazed at such heat of passion in the man, and she looked at him for a moment, glanced at the door and turned to look at him with a vague expression of sympathy. She seemed to be thinking, 'What a pity that he is not someone else.' But she quickly understood that her silence could be misinterpreted, and she hastened to say in the friendliest possible tone, 'Well, enough of this, Mr Celzani. I have already told you my feelings. You are a good-hearted person. You'll find another who suits you (as you certainly deserve). You are deceived about me; I am not as you perhaps imagine. I am not affectionate. I myself have the heart of a man. I would not make a good wife. You must see that I mean what I say and get used to it… and give me the receipt. I don't wish to stay here any longer.'

Celzani stayed where he was as if frozen. But the terror of remaining alone in the house as well as the desperation of that refusal in his heart was suddenly made real to him, and it caused him to resort to one last desolate attempt at begging. 'At least take some time to answer! Think about it again! Don't give me a final no!'

Miss Pedani began to get impatient, and she took a step forwards, and reached out her hand to take the receipt. The secretary instinctively grabbed her hand, and all at once he fell to his knees as if he had lost his balance. Blinded and beseeching, he clung furiously to the young lady's knees as he rubbed his face convulsively against her dress. In a flash, however, two energetic hands loosened his intertwined fingers and with a quick and manly push, threw the poor startled man away from her.

'Mr Celzani,' she said severely, but with a tone that was more annoyed than scornful. 'I will not allow you to take such liberties with me.' Then she added after a pause, 'That goes for now and forever.'

But the secretary was deaf to her words. The overwhelming pain of her refusal, the shame and the terror of the future were stifled in him by the deep and violent sensations of that embrace, which revealed mysterious treasures that overcame his conscious thoughts and which left him feeling as if he had just been in contact with some superhuman agency. His sensations returned, and he saw her drawing near to the door, and with unsteady and impulsive steps he reached her, but he stopped just short of her. She already had her hand on the doorknob; she withdrew it and looked at him with an indulgent smile, and then she offered her hand in hearty friendship, and in that one action she removed all sense of tenderness. The secretary understood all too well, and gave her his own lifeless hand.

Becoming serious once more, she said, 'We understand one another, then. Never again.'

He replied mechanically as if unconscious of his words, 'Never again.'

He did not see her out. As she crossed the antechamber, the teacher heard a long muffled sob as if someone were weeping between two clenched fists and then a sudden stamping of the feet, similar to that made by a recalcitrant mule. She left shaking her head with compassion.

After that day Celzani was another person. He no longer waited for the teacher on the stairway, he started smoking Virginia cigars, he frequented the nearby Café Monviso, and he attended the Alfieri Theatre. He affected a more casual attitude. As for his work as secretary, he threw himself into it with a hitherto unseen industriousness; it was as if his uncle's property had suddenly trebled. He increased his eccentricity to the point of changing his habitual black silk tie to one that was navy blue, thus making him look even more audacious. All the tenants noticed the transformation. He was sometimes heard to hum in the stairwell, and he was seen to go up or down the steps in little jumps; the tenants would meet him in the street, gesticulating in the company of young men of his own age with whom they had not seen him before and so completely unlike his former state as a would-be priest. Only Ginoni knew the reason for this metamorphosis and took pleasure in it, as he said to the secretary when he encountered him, 'The spell has been broken, and the yoke is shattered on the ground,' or, 'O Nissa, I can breathe at last.'[32] 'Good work, secretary!'

Celzani responded to these with a humorous expression as if to say, 'That's all in the past.' And so it went for the entire month of March… after which he fell back in love more hopelessly than ever. But, great God, what was he to do? In the early days of the new season Miss Pedani had worn a lightweight woollen suit of brown trimmed in black silk; it was extremely simple: just a plain little thing that could not have cost her more than thirty lire and was probably ill-made to boot. But the best and most wonderful dressmaker of all was the wearer herself, who filled the garment with amazing curves that were more seductive than even a sculptor could have imagined for his goddess. There were now days when she returned from the gymnasium and the hours spent in the fresh air and sunshine combined with the exercise caused her flesh to give off the warm glow of full-orbed youth; it was the freshness of a swimmer's body that has just left the water, rather like the intoxicating fragrance given off by a flowering tree. Walking past Rev. Celzani at a brisk pace, she said to him, 'Hello,' with her strong, deep oboe-like voice which seemed to drip with unintentional voluptuousness and which cut him to the quick. After poor Celzani had been subjected to three or four of these encounters, he was lost once more. He left the Café Monviso, the theatre, his friends, his Virginia cigars, the footraces in Turin and the casual attitudes. After only one month nothing remained to mark his audacious rebellion except the navy blue cravat.

But during that month he had meditated, and the fruit of his meditations was that he entered a new period, and he changed his lovemaking tactics. He strove to give his passion the appearance of a tranquil friendship. No more ambushes, no more supplicating gazes – there were neither nervous greetings nor silent adoration. He waited for the teacher on the stairway and accompanied her, chatting with her on a variety of subjects: philosophising about the weather or school schedules, about repairs that had to be made, a tenant or some unimportant trifle. He wanted simply to talk to her and to entertain her so that she would become accustomed to his company, and to persuade her that from now on it was possible to be with him without having to listen to his previous declarations of love. And in this he was successful. At first, however, she had confused suspicions that there were ulterior motives hidden behind his new behaviour; but on the whole, he was calmer, and they could talk about things. So much so that when that mad love was removed from him, she found him to be polite and quite a nice fellow, and she did not avoid his company. In this way they began to establish a certain familiarity between themselves.

This familiarity was made easier because of a new declaration of war by Miss Zibelli which allowed her friend to go out alone. This came about because of an amusing incident: these two friends were to have met for the first time together with the blond gymnastics teacher from La Generala prison in the Piazza Solferino.[33] He had stopped to chat with the two ladies, and after only a few words, he had clarified his misunderstanding: until that time he had mistaken Miss Zibelli for Miss Pedani (who was known to him only by reputation and whom he admired for her articles). Miss Zibelli saw immediately that he had turned his attention from her to Pedani, but with double the respect and admiration of which she had at first been the object. She was completely devastated by this discovery, she spent several horrible days being comforted by her friend from morning to night, but afterwards she took up religion with great ardour. She went to church every morning, drew closer in friendship with the devout ladies on the first floor, wore a black veil over her face, made up her mind to fast on Fridays and Saturdays, and spent all of her spare time studying devotional books which she read aloud even at night.

Thanks to an extraordinary event, the jealousy over her friend's literary and gymnastic triumphs that had started to build in the preceding days was destined to get even worse. The Minister of Public Instruction, Guido Baccelli, came to Turin at that time.[34] He arrived unannounced one morning along with the mayor, an alderman and a numerous procession of officials while Miss Pedani was in the middle of her gymnastics lesson. Someone else might have been befuddled by this visit, but she was not bothered at all, and after lining up her students, she had them perform their rhythmic exercises with such variety, precision and vigour of command, that (whether because of the exercises or because of her personal beauty) the Minister lavished upon her the warmest praise, initiating a conversation with her on English gymnastic methods, after which he was even more impressed than he had been by the exercises. This event was reported in the newspapers that printed her name and was a great honour. But Miss Zibelli was not the only one who was made jealous: the teacher, Mr Fassi, completely lost his temper. Miss Pedani had also at that time been named gymnastics instructor to the nuns of Saint Vincent-de-Paul of Cottolengo.[35] Such an unheard-of succession of good luck could no longer be understood unless it could be explained by some sort of secret protection. Now the teacher got it into his head that the one who was responsible for all of her favours was old Mr Celzani, who had been influenced by his nephew, and he could hardly wait to tell everyone about this.

'It is shameful,' he said out of the blue one day, 'that while there are gymnastics instructors who kill themselves working for twenty years without ever being able to obtain recognition or the rewards that come from notoriety, there is one who has elbowed her way in and has got all the honours simply because she wears a skirt. It is a revolting business which I will denounce to the press.'

The secretary pretended not to understand. But this pretence merely reassured the teacher that he was right, so much so that although for his own interests Fassi kept up the appearance of friendship with Miss Pedani, he no longer regarded her as a friend (and his wife did the same). And thus there were already three who had become Maria Pedani's sworn enemies.

Rev. Celzani continued fearlessly and persistently to attain his goals by trying to get into Miss Pedani's good graces. He gave her real pleasure one day when he brought her an issue of *The Trieste Gymnast* which he had obtained quite by chance and which contained an article on the Pyrrhic Dance.[36] Another time he brought her an issue of *The Tribune* that his uncle had received, in which was reported the negative analysis given by the City of Rome's Office of Hygiene to the principals of all schools examining the question of the advantages and disadvantages of having students stand with their arms crossed. The teacher greatly appreciated this little gift, saying that she had already addressed the subject in an article. But the secretary was prepared to offer her many other surprises as well. For some time he had been attempting to initiate certain discussions with her that he had been preparing, but had not yet dared. One day he dared: since she had said that she attended a course of anatomy, he replied timidly, 'Anatomy – that is good, because without studying that, one can't understand the value – physiologically speaking – of a single exercise, and without this, the exercises cannot be classified – physiologically speaking – in the most useful order.'

The teacher stared at him in amazement, and she approved. It was the first step. Another day he took heart and asked her what she thought about the issue of apparatuses. Once more, this question pleasantly surprised her, and she answered him. She did not agree with those who wanted to misuse them and whose goal was to turn the gymnasium into an acrobatic circus; it was this sort of thing that alarmed families and was really quite dangerous. She likewise disagreed with those of the opposite side who exaggerated the drawbacks and who wanted to abolish them altogether. But where would we end up if we continued down this road? At infantile play, which will not develop in children that most important quality, *physical courage*, which is so necessary to all, and without which they will not succeed later in either regular or acrobatic exercises. If not that, then it will be at the price of painful attempts and a ridiculous appearance.

Rev. Celzani approved with repeated nods of his head. 'I too am convinced,' he said, searching for the right words, 'that the complete development of all the limbs cannot be obtained if not with the help of apparatuses. The ones whose usefulness is questionable can be left out, but those that have a demonstrable, err... *anthropological* usefulness are, according to me, indispensable.'

'At last!' exclaimed the teacher as she looked at him curiously. 'Are you not also of the opinion that one should allow the individual teacher to follow her own ideas and opinions when she chooses the number and methods of using the apparatuses?'

'There can be no doubt of it,' replied Rev. Celzani seriously. 'If this is not done, it removes from the teacher every encouragement to study ways of making original combinations in the various orders and classifications – one can tick them off on the fingers of one's hand: anatomical, pedagogical, collective, individual, and so on; and besides, who has more experience and has done more research…?'

The teacher turned to look at him with a mixture of amazement and pleasure. Urged on by greater curiosity, she stopped on the stairway. 'And which would they be,' she asked him, 'the apparatuses that you would deem essential?'

'The apparatuses that I would deem essential,' Rev. Celzani replied with the tone of a child at catechism, and raising his hand to count once more on his fingers, 'they would be climbing poles, balance beam (but not raised up too high, otherwise it becomes useless), the horizontal bar, naturally the parallel bars and the inclined board. At most, I would leave aside only a few exercises: the flying trapeze, for example.'

'What?' she asked with professorial sharpness, 'Are you also among those who consider the trapeze to be dangerous?'

'No, I was mistaken,' the secretary answered. 'The trapeze should really be retained. Actually, what dangers are there? At the worst there are a few sprains. So we are in agreement on this, too.'

'We agree on everything, then,' the teacher exclaimed with satisfaction. 'To tell the truth, one cannot have good sense and think otherwise.' Then curiosity got the better of her as they were passing through the door, and she asked him with an unusual smile, 'Have you been studying these things for a long time?' The secretary blushed and made an indefinite gesture without saying anything. But after that day he returned to the subject at every meeting.

His uncle possessed some books on gymnastics that had been presented to him by the authors during his tenure as deputy-alderman in charge of public instruction and a few bundles of *The Arezzo Gymnast* that had been sent to him several years earlier by a Tuscan friend. Rev. Celzani read every scrap in order to prepare himself for certain questions and certain replies, and thus be able to keep the conversation going. He had finally found the key to the teacher's heart, and he greatly admired the engineer's perspicacity. Now, when they spoke of these things, the teacher detained him on every stair or two, and this afforded him a deliciously easy opportunity to admire her as never before, and he memorised all the folds, buttons and ribbons of that awful brown-coloured dress. He discovered some of her little mannerisms that he had never before seen; he studied her white teeth one by one; he made real voyages of exploration with his eyes that ranged all over her form, and he became so deeply absorbed while making these loving investigations that he forgot to answer or he answered at the wrong time. The problem was that while he was playing this little game, he very soon lost control of himself, and this was antithetical to his goals. Little by little he began to think that she was transferring to him the affection that she showed for the subject of their conversations. It seemed to him that he was greeted, observed and listened to in a completely different way from before. He felt a slight shudder once more when she looked him in the eye, and he feared that she might discover the cause. Two or three times he was on the point of giving himself away by grabbing her beautiful arm out of the air as she demonstrated an exercise on an imaginary hanging beam. He stopped himself, however. But he took such courage that he decided to attempt another proposal that was more elaborately prepared than the other; he chose the first day of May, when she would come to him to bring the rent. He believed that this time she would at least not give him an absolute rejection. There was a bond between them. It seemed to him that the idea of marrying him because she could have an intelligent partner for her conversations, a perpetual mirror to reflect her dominant passion and a kind of intellectual secretary, would weigh heavily in her decision. Besides, he had something held in reserve that would give him an extra impetus: the revelation of a little secret that (because he was a bit ashamed) he had kept jealously guarded from the entire house for some time.

But, alas, it was no longer a secret from anyone. The day before he had intended to make his third proposal, the eldest Ginoni son came home at dinnertime and blurted out some news that caused everyone to burst out laughing.

'Papa,' he said, crossing his arms on his chest, 'do you want to hear something incredible? Mr Celzani is going to the gymnasium!'

But after the laughter, there came exclamations of disbelief. And yet, he had seen the man enter the gymnasium in the Corso Umberto at opening time along with the other members. There could not be a shadow of a doubt.

The hopes that Rev. Celzani had cherished for the first of May were dashed by an unexpected event. In order to avoid the visits from his tenants, his uncle left every first of the month to spend the day away from home, but on this day he stayed at home, ensconced in his usual spot in his armchair as if he were waiting for them. His nephew, who had done everything to prepare the ground for battle, was in a dreadful fit. He had hoped all along that the old man would decide to leave, but by eleven he had given up all hope and restlessly paced around the room. But suddenly a comforting thought flashed upon him: his uncle was curious to see Miss Pedani at closer range and to converse with her since they had had little contact except to greet one another on the stairway, and this was a sign of good intentions. Ever since his visit with the superintendent, his uncle had spoken no more of the affair, but Rev. Celzani knew that his uncle was not unaware of the resolute persistence of his feelings. Who knows? Perhaps the old man had actually planned it this way. And then his spite switched to impatience. She would probably come at half past one, as she had the last time. At one o'clock the commendatore was seated at the desk with his majestic white head resting on the back of the armchair and his blue eyes staring at the ceiling. Whether it was premeditated or not, he made as if to go away and leave the field to his nephew when the servant announced Miss Pedani, but then he changed his mind.

The teacher entered and it seemed that she did not regret finding the landlord there, perhaps because it would make a new declaration of love (which she had feared) out of the question. Old Celzani was particularly courteous when it came to his tenants, and when it came to the fair sex, he assumed an extraordinarily respectful and dignified demeanour. He arose and bowed with closed eyes in front of the young lady; then he sat down again and insisted that she also be seated. The secretary took the money and wrote the receipt with an unsteady hand, constantly shooting clandestine glances up at both of them. He was seized by boyish emotions; it was as if Miss Pedani had just been introduced to the family and the negotiations for marriage would be decided on the spot.

'And so, my dear young lady,' intoned the commendatore with a dignity that was tempered with a ceremonious smile after the secretary had once more handed the paper to the teacher, 'how are gymnastics these days?'

It was evident that he wanted to make her speak at length. The teacher replied that it was always the same: there was a certain amount of prejudice to be overcome with the families of the students as well as with the authorities; because of which the teachers must maintain a constant struggle, which was naturally to the detriment of their instruction.

'This is especially so in female gymnastics,' said the old man gravely.

'Especially in female gymnastics,' repeated Miss Pedani, who then became more animated. 'And for a world of reasons (none of which are logical). No doubt you are aware of these things. I am not saying that considering today's prevailing views, it is possible to put Baumann's more advanced concepts into effect immediately – such as expecting both boys and girls to perform the same gymnastics – but those opponents who want to reduce all participation by girls in gymnastics, well that's really going too far.'

The commendatore lowered his eyelids in a sign of assent. In his view, the real problem was teaching gymnastics in order to give exercise demonstrations and for showing off in front of visiting officials, which leads to excessive rectitude and a reluctance to move freely.

'How true!' remarked the teacher passionately. 'It is exactly what I've always said.' As she warmed to the subject, she either forgot or refused to believe what the engineer had said, and with the naivety of a monomaniac she forged ahead to the ex-alderman's favourite topic. 'They tell us that girls shouldn't do the same exercises that boys do. But I say those exercises are either healthy or they are not. If they are, how then can we eliminate them for girls without any solid reason? Here is my point: girls need only perform their exercises in front of their teachers or their mothers, so if we eliminate the public exhibitions that cause all the problems, we will eliminate all the difficulties at the same time.'

The old man approved. Actually, according to him the exhibitions should be left alone, but he did not say so. He contented himself with making a general observation on the great need that there was, especially for girls, for more energetic gymnastics, more like those that were currently used in Germany. The new generation in his opinion left a lot to be desired.

He had plucked the teacher's most resonant string.

'A lot to be desired!' she exclaimed. 'It is all too clear that you, sir, are not in a position to have a precise understanding. But we who can see our girls clearly and who have the duty of examining them, of touching them – we can grasp the situation, and we understand the absolute necessity of what you have just said. If you could only see it for yourself…'

The commendatore half-closed his eyes and became deeply attentive.

'If you could see,' continued the teacher, 'what poor forms they have. I am not speaking of those who have real physical disabilities, but rather of those who have fairly good constitutions without either physical defects or any diagnosed infirmities, and yet we must pity them. They are growing quickly, but only the skeleton has lengthened; the muscular system has not developed proportionally. They do not have shoulders, arms or bosoms. Truthfully, they need not worry about flattening their "forward parts" as mothers often fear. After only the slightest exertions they are gasping for breath, and there are some who faint. They seem like children who have recently suffered from a dreadful illness. It is vexing to see the sort of puritanical restrictions that are put on such girls who should be doing nothing but gymnastics from morning till night!'

'What sort of restrictions are applied… generally speaking?' asked the commendatore as he looked at his fingernails.

'Oh, of every sort,' replied Miss Pedani. 'They want to greatly restrict the exercises for the abduction and raising of the legs, and I know not what else. Then on the parallel bars and on the vaulting board as well as on the wall bars – all of the exercises in which it is necessary to lift the lower limbs. The bigger girls are forbidden to use either the climbing rope or the pole. What am I to do?' And she kept on going.

The commendatore listened with his blue eyes staring at the ceiling as if absorbed in divine contemplations, slowly nodding his head in agreement.

'And the thing is,' the teacher continued, 'what makes us more and more enthusiastic about our ideas is to see the progress that is achieved with the little that is allowed. You cannot believe the change that can be seen in the girls from twelve years of age onwards after one month of gymnastics, and so much more among those that are thin and anaemic because of illnesses suffered in infancy or acquired from lymphangitis. After one month the colour returns to their cheeks, which were once so pale, the arms become fuller, the back straightens and the muscles develop. At times when they are seen from behind, they are no longer recognisable; they have become "young ladies". They have acquired that elegance and quickness of movement that constitutes true aesthetic beauty, especially in the lower limbs: it is an amazing development. It is truly a comforting thing.'

Indeed, it was also comforting to the commendatore, who continued to follow his train of thought. And he asked a question that seemed to arise from the depths of his meditation. 'Besides all that,' he said, 'you will no doubt have a particular satisfaction from those few who have an exceptional physical aptitude for gymnastics and an enthusiasm equal to your own; because among the many that you encounter, some must be like this.' Half closing his eyes, he then turned to stare upwards as if to savour the answer.

'Oh, those. Yes,' replied the teacher excitedly. 'There are a few of them. And at this point, I can tell at the first glance, at the first time that they are introduced to me; but it's not always that easy. That is because those who are well formed or who have a slender appearance do not always have the best aptitudes. It all depends on the more or less harmonious structure of the limbs. There are some fat girls, for example, whom one would assume to be heavy and clumsy, but instead they have an agility and elasticity that would amaze you. Mr Celzani, you really should come to visit us at the Institute for Military Daughters during recreation time.'

Old Celzani closed his eyes.

'Because,' continued the teacher, 'the rules of gymnastics can restrict the movements more than one would want, but after the lessons the best girls can do what they please. There are about a dozen girls at the school of San Domenico between the ages of fourteen and eighteen who could perform a show that is worthy of the theatre – real acrobats who can do turns on the horizontal bar that would make your head swim and high jumps of a metre and a half from the incline board.' Then she added with a smile, 'It's a good thing that there are no spectators. I could describe to you arms and legs of steel and narrow waists that twist like metal springs – I can assure you, it is a beautiful sight to behold. And I tell you that we could do as much for the others… That would be a blessing!'

Yes, that would have been a blessing; the commendatore was convinced of it more than anyone. And after a brief meditation, he suddenly collected himself and voiced his thoughts. 'We must continue to hope, my dear Miss Pedani, that little by little these things will come to pass. Good causes will always be victorious in the end. Meanwhile, resistance falls away on all sides. And you must continue resolutely on your mission, which is a sacred duty, for the well-being of our poor young girls; we all owe you a debt of gratitude.'

The teacher thanked him as she arose; the old man also got up (cutting off his nephew) and politely accompanied her to the door where he made a deep bow.

The secretary had been standing apart from them this whole time but had not missed a single syllable of their conversation as he watched the two faces alternately. Afterwards, he was overjoyed at the thought that the teacher must have made an excellent impression on his uncle.

The old man returned and stood in the middle of the room, and running his hand over his stately white hair, said in a paternal way, almost speaking to himself, 'A very nice girl.' And he remained absorbed in his own thoughts.

'So then,' the young man asked nervously, 'you no longer have any objections?'

The uncle did not appear to understand what he meant right away. Then, after he understood, he answered carelessly, 'For my part, I have none. Only,' he added, looking at his nephew from head to toe, 'do you have her consent?'

The secretary reverted to his priestly pose with one hand grasping the other, and lowering his sparkling eyes, he answered with appropriate humility, 'I can only hope.'

'We shall see,' said his uncle, examining his nephew once more. He then sat down in his armchair with his neck resting on the chair back and half-closed his eyes. He soon became lost in his thoughts again.

Rev. Celzani was happy. Thereafter, the way would be entirely free, and after that visit the teacher must also be more favourably disposed towards him than ever. With his usual caution, he planned on posing a test question, and then he would make the final move if the first attempt was well received. This test question could be asked anywhere. He therefore expected to ask her on the staircase, but this was not to be. Miss Zibelli had reconciled with her friend for the hundredth time; their latest rift had been caused for the usual reason. After Ginoni's eldest son saw his successive assaults rejected by Miss Pedani, he had started doing little favours for Miss Zibelli; this was done partly in retaliation and partly out of childish malice since he believed that he could wring love from disdain. This was not a formal wooing; it was rather a kind of semi-serious foolishness consisting of friendly conversations, small bouquets, and tender handholding when he encountered her by herself. Although Miss Zibelli neither put much faith in these demonstrations, nor did she understand the reason for them; she still enjoyed them as a caress to her ego, as a recreation, and as a pleasant retreat for her imagination. For this reason she made up with Miss Pedani, and every time she thought that there was no chance of meeting young Ginoni, she would again accompany her friend whenever they came and went as she had done before. Because of this Mr Celzani failed in his various interceptions.

Once when he was about to ambush his beautiful prey all alone, Professor Padalocchi left his house and stopped Miss Pedani to complain about his usual difficulty with breathing and to tell her that the arm rotations that she had suggested tired him out too much. After thinking for a bit, the teacher advised him to read aloud, telling him that the acceleration of respiration with this exercise was calculated to be 1.26. She warned him, however, to loosen his tie, and then she explained to him the advantages of this. The secretary hoped that this was an end of it, but the blasted old man then asked for a clarification on the flexing movements of Schreber's gymnastics, and Celzani had to give up on his plans.

Another time she was alone and had almost reached the bottom of the stairs while the secretary was just coming in, but then Ginoni, who was also entering, appeared behind him. After Celzani had resumed his lovelorn look, Ginoni decided (half out of benevolence and half in jest) to act as his protector. But this time all he provided was discomfort.

'Miss Pedani,' he said with great seriousness, placing a hand on the secretary's shoulder, 'I'd like to introduce you to one of the most assiduous and capable acrobats of the Turin Gymnasium.'

Celzani trembled, denied it, reddened and flushed with annoyance; he wished that he could run away and hide and bestow his heartsick feelings on the impertinent fellow next to him. But the teacher made an exclamation of joyful admiration, looking at him as if to find the changes that gymnastics had wrought upon his person. At that precise moment he had assumed his usual priestly pose, but she thought that she could detect something livelier in his gaze. Despite it all, she feared a joke once more.

'You see that he does not deny it twice,' said the engineer. 'You may believe it, Miss: the fact that you have got *Reverend* Celzani to go to the gymnasium will resound as the greatest of your triumphs!'

That 'Reverend' once more cut Celzani to the quick. Even so, when he saw on the young lady's face a smile of such sincere pleasure without the slightest hint of ridicule, he took heart. Yes, the moment had arrived, and it would do well not to put it off for even one day more. Indeed, he set his plan in motion that very evening before nightfall, at a time when he knew that Miss Zibelli was out. Using the pretext of going to see if there had been a problem with the drinking water pipe, he entered Miss Pedani's apartment.

He hoped to be received in her private room, but instead he was greeted in the parlour and was kept standing. She was wearing her blue striped gymnastics blouse, which set off her shoulders nicely, and a white skirt with an ink stain on the knee. For the first time she seemed a bit embarrassed, and this surprised Celzani. The embarrassment, however, was not caused so much by his visit (whose purpose she had already guessed), as by the absolute certainty that she had seen the serving girl standing behind the door and that she would not miss a single syllable of their conversation. She was therefore forced to be brief and almost cruel in her words, but she tried to temper that cruelty with her facial expressions.

After speaking loudly about the pipe, Celzani then spoke softly and trembling, 'Miss, I have come for the last time to ask you if you are still of the same mind.'

She looked at him with a kindly expression, glanced at the door and repeated with a hint of regret his own words, 'Still of the same mind…'

Celzani paled and asked even more softly, 'Are you… in… flexible?'

The teacher turned to look at the door, and bending forward a little, her face a picture of pity, she answered, 'Yes.'

The secretary brought his hand to his forehead and covered his eyes. That answer had paralysed him; he could not speak. The silence grew longer. He could not remain like this. The teacher did not know what to say either, and she made a small gesture of apprehension which he noticed.

'Well, then,' he said, 'I must go.'

She did not reply. He moved, and when he was at the door, he turned back, his face distorted with sorrow and with a desperate tone of voice that would have caused an indifferent spectator to burst out laughing, he said, 'Well then, there is nothing I can do about the water pipe!'

The absurd contrast between his voice and the words touched the young lady's heart more than any supplication; she was tempted to say something to make him feel better, but her conscience forbade her from deluding him, and she merely said with an affectionate and compassionate smile, 'No, Mr Celzani. There is nothing that you can do.'

He replied with a sigh in his throat, 'My respects to you!' And he left.

Then he despaired because by then he loved her with his whole heart marked by a mixture of ardent sensuality and childish tenderness. Continually present in his thoughts was that embrace that had made him drunk with pleasure and the recollection of their pleasant conversations. Celzani recalled so much trepidation, so much hope and so much disappointment that it seemed he had spent half his life in such misery. This time he did not even try to rebel against his passion as he had the last time because he felt that it was no longer possible. No, at the price of any torment, he had to keep on seeing her, speaking to her, following her like a lapdog, scurrying between her feet at every step. He had to continue to inhale the perfume of her youth and to hear her deep voice, to take pleasure at least in her pity, and with his heart and his flesh continually under her gaze to torture himself with his imagination. The torments embittered him, but he sought them out.

With the approach of summer she wore fewer clothes, allowing her form to become more in evidence, and this drove him to distraction. He went back up to the attic to kneel among the dust and the dried leaves with his face to the dormer window and his gaze upon her. She gave her lessons with an open bodice, showing her wide, bare shoulders and her stupendous arms. Celzani was in a state of torment. Sometimes he could not even see her, but he listened to her voice for an hour as she called out commands, 'On your stomach, on your back, palms forward, palms inward, swing both arms simultaneously…' These resonated in his soul like exclamations of love. He no longer slept at night so that he could hear all the noises from the floor above, the slightest of which made him start as if he had felt her footsteps on his body. His brain was weary, and in that feverish weakness he imagined stratagems and rash activities in order to spy on her: from holes in the attic and little openings in the wall to a complicated series of mirrors and unlikely lookouts. He had arrived at such a state of excitement that he no longer noticed the neighbours when he waited for her; he went out, came in, went up the stairs at all hours of the day. He followed her in the street, waited for her in the courtyard, seized all the lamest pretexts to speak to her, and offered her all sorts of odd services no matter who was around. He no longer seemed like a suitor but a slave. He exasperated her with a smouldering and yet humble gaze that did not ask for love in return, but merely compassion. He repeated echo-like her every word and the commonest and most unimportant of her sentences; he was content to enfold her form, her talent and her increasing fame in nothing more than excessive admiration. And yet he restrained himself in her presence, but only until she had passed; he then put a hand over his mouth as he watched her from behind, and in that way he stifled the cry of love and desire that issued from him in the form of a mournful, muffled sigh. Unlike the other times, he hardly dared to fix his imagination on the bliss of total possession, because as soon as he removed the last veil from his living idol, it would open up a luminous abyss of voluptuousness to his mind, and then his only refuge would be to flee in terror from looming madness.

And so in order to calm himself, he turned to thoughts of affection; he imagined the bridegroom's new house, he furnished it and he imagined affectionate scenes; he saw a white cradle. But passion attacked suddenly even in this refuge: he saw another cradle, then ten, twenty, a vast throng that issued forth from her embrace, and this was still not enough for him. The poor man's imagination was still tormented by that person who remained always before him, fresh and powerful like the image of immortal youth and eternal voluptuousness. His ardour grew day by day because of the familiar friendship that she offered him, believing that he had resigned himself to her refusal.

The entire day was not long enough for that varying and dizzying succession of daydreams, of hurried trips to the dormer, of five-minute conversations for which he had to wait half an hour, of sudden and solitary impulses of tenderness and anguish from which he suffered (and almost enjoyed the suffering). He could not concentrate on his job, his memory failed him in all his affairs, and his life began to unravel. His very health began to be affected; his face took on a new aspect that was odd, childish and frightening while at the same time marked by a great goodness that was both ingenuous and stupefied – like a man intent on the perpetual adoration of an elusive phantom in the air.

Engineer Ginoni, who observed all of this *crescit eundo*[37] with a curious and knowing eye, encountered Miss Pedani one fine day in the court. He stood five steps in front of her and mockingly threatened her with his cane. Then he came nearer and translated his act into words. 'Ah! Heartless woman! Do you not realise that because of you poor Rev. Celzani is losing his reason?' The teacher did not understand. 'No, really,' the engineer continued, 'he is becoming quite unhinged.' And then he told her what he had heard from the commendatore.

For some time now the secretary had not left the house, and business affairs had gone downhill rapidly; the tenants of the other house in Vanchiglia had come to raise Cain with the landlord because they had not received any replies to their requests. The good secretary had been fined twice because he was late in paying the registry taxes. 'This,' he added, 'is what comes of gymnastics! Behold the evil effects of exercise of the muscular system upon the functions of the brain! Just three days ago, poor Mr Celzani was severely bamboozled in the sale of eight hundredweight of kindling and firewood from his uncle's farms because he made a mistake in addition that cost the old man 112.75 lire. The old man was furious and gave his nephew a terrible scolding. If the secretary ever does that again, his uncle has decided *ipso facto* to dispense with his services and to send him away to be miserable in someone else's house. And you – *cold-hearted seductress* – in this way you dared to ruin a poor young gentleman!'

Miss Pedani did not smile. Indeed, she felt bad about the situation. Staring at the ground and absorbed in thought, she said, 'I am sorry to hear this.' Then she added, 'But I am not to blame for it.'

'There is the problem in a nutshell!' laughingly replied the engineer. 'For if you had been in the wrong for something, you would be obliged to rectify it. And then, consider for a bit the advantages! The secretary would not lose his mind; the commendatore would not lose his secretary – the poor secretary! A man with a heart of gold, a profoundly honest man, the cream of all the would-be priests that God has put on the earth. He only has the misfortune to aspire to a perfection of figures, and as we all know, only a few privileged souls are allowed to attain perfection.' Here he burst out laughing. 'Ah, what a marvel! To think that you have sent Rev. Celzani to the pommel horse!'

The teacher grew pensive.

'But enough of this,' added the engineer. 'So long as he doesn't jump off the pommel horse and into the Po!'

'Oh, my dear sir,' said Miss Pedani with a smile, 'Mr Celzani is not the sort of man who would do such things.'

'Ah, my dear Miss,' replied Ginoni, 'even the most reasonable and even-tempered man in this world is nothing but water in a glass. Whether it overflows or not depends on the strength of the effervescent powder that is poured into it by passion.'

With these words, he bid her good day, and she proceeded to the staircase deep in thought.

But she did not remain long in her funk, for a great gymnastics meet was taking place in Frankfurt, and the reports that arrived hour by hour were a powerful nourishment for her dominating passion. Every newspaper brought her new details and heightened her enthusiasm. She saw the arrival of the delegations in the city as they were received by the burgermeister and by an immense crowd of citizens; she saw the grand triumphal procession of forty thousand gymnasts from every country in the world: boys, old men, and men in the flower of their youth, all waving hundreds of little pennants.

They were accompanied by two thousand singers from the choral societies who advanced down the flag-bedecked streets under triumphal arches and amid houses decorated with crowns and garlands and all under a rain of flowers. She saw the immense gymnasium with its colossal statue of Germania; and the infinite number of apparatuses, the twenty thousand spectators who applauded the prodigies of strength, skill and daring. She saw pictures showing the virile physique of Meller, the winner of the first prize who waved his crown of oak leaves to the hurrahs of the populace. She imagined that army of muscular young men who wandered throughout the old city where they could see on every street corner the portrait of Turnvater Jahn; where the athletes can mix in brotherhood with the citizenry and they are surrounded by the most famous gymnasiarchs, the most gifted writers, doctors, reformers all speaking in twenty different tongues. It was everything that she loved and admired, where everyone was inebriated with the regeneration of the human race, with the breath of youth and the grandeur that hung in the air as if it were a massive ancient spectacle from Corinth or Delphi. Oh, how beautiful and grand it all was! She thought also of being able to compete, no matter how minuscule her contribution in her small field, of preparing a similar festival in her own country, of broadcasting her confidence in the wonderful effects of physical education and of exciting others to spread the good news of a new era – all this inflamed her heart, illuminated all of her faculties and tripled her strength for the job.

She was at that time in the process of preparing a speech on this subject to be given at the next national conference of elementary teachers which was to be held in Turin, and since she had been successful with a series of articles in *The Field of Mars* in which she hotly defended creating a company of volunteer women fire fighters in all the large cities, she readied herself to lecture on this theme in a hall at the Archimedes School. In the meantime she received from every side encouragement, letters of congratulation, propositions and questions from eager gymnasts, and she replied to all of these. Certainly, her strongest motivation for this whole job was derived from her firm and ardent determination to do good. She had been aware of this feeling from her earliest youth, but with her growing fame and public praise, a previously unknown sentiment of personal satisfaction began to get mixed in – an idea of ambition that she did not dare to admit to herself and with which came a novel difficulty that appears with the first consciousness of fame. It is a certain bitterness that comes from not knowing in whom one can pour the overflow of one's intellectual and moral life; it was this that agitated her and that overcame the native strength of her temperament, and it made her feel more like a woman than ever before. For her, who never considered leaving her humble obscurity, that faint buzz around her name that could be heard in her little corner of the world was glory, and glory is solitude. When she felt that solitude during breaks in her work, on days in which her friend was not speaking to her, her thoughts sometimes ran to poor Rev. Celzani, not as a lover, but as a friend; then she would stop a while with her pen-holder resting on her lower lip, and smile benevolently as she recalled his image. He loved her, there was no doubt of it, and she well understood that his was one of those passions that was destined to last an entire lifetime. If only…

Miss Pedani gave her lecture on female volunteer fire fighters. She had not chosen the right time, and there were very few people in attendance; there were around thirty ladies and a group of students, but among those who were there she made a great hit, as much by the singularity of the subject as by the originality and vivacity of her speaking style. One of the first to run up and shake her hand was young Ginoni who greeted her with great sauciness as if nothing had happened between them; he even sported a mischievous smile which (to her regret) allowed her to see that he was back to his old tricks again. In fact, seeing her in public, admired and applauded, his fancy for her grew even stronger, fed by the flames of vanity. The thought of the exquisite feast of selfishness that he would taste when he had succeeded in winning her, aroused within him an irresistible tickle whenever he saw her in such circumstances. Since he did not know her very well, and since he was an impetuous and lighthearted young man, he believed in making frontal attacks, so he tried a new tactic.

The next day at the time when she left alone, he waited for her under the landing of the first floor. It was raining, and the stairway was dark – perfect for his purposes. In order to start up a conversation he had bought at Berry's a portrait of Meller, the winner of the first prize at Frankfurt; within only a few days thousands of these photographs had been reproduced and sent all over Europe. When he heard her coming down, he climbed up towards her.

She was truly beautiful that day. Still a bit excited from the small triumph of the previous evening, she was dressed in dark colours with a large black hat that admirably crowned her strong and slender form. The young man raised his hat, and with casual joy he revealed the photograph to her. 'Miss,' he said, 'will you permit me to offer you a portrait that you might perhaps be curious to see?'

She drew near his face cautiously, but after she had read the name, she made an exclamation of pleasure, 'Meller!' She took the portrait and went over to the wall in order to see better by the weak light that came from the little window in the stairway. The young man moved in close to her as if to look at him also; he stuck out his chin just above her shoulder and began to give some explanations in a low voice, pointing with the index finger of his right hand.

'Here is a true German type. Look at the structure of his skull; look at that mouth. And yet if he were not famous, one would never guess that he was the finest gymnast in Germany. Doesn't he seem more like a mild-mannered professor of literature? Won't you ever give me a word of comfort? Will you always be so indifferent to me? Will you always have a heart that…'

The switch from one question to another had been so natural that the teacher had not immediately noticed it, but she understood soon enough after feeling the young man's cheek next to her own and an arm around her waist. She freed herself with an abrupt movement while saying, 'Mr Ginoni, this is a dirty trick!'

The young man drew back in order to make a humorous reply, but he refrained and his face grew darker when he saw above him at the head of the stairs the anguished face of the secretary, who descended quickly and who also carried a portrait of Meller! All the same, young Ginoni was not dissatisfied to find a way out of this embarrassing situation.

'What are you doing here?' asked the secretary who had stopped there and was staring daggers at the young man.

'You haven't come here to raise the rent, have you?'

The secretary could only repeat the teacher's words while trembling with rage, 'This trick is dirty!'

'Good heavens!' replied the young man as the teacher slowly moved away from him. 'There's a perfect echo in here (except for moving the adjective). But beware, the words that you have spoken; I will take them in a completely different way.'

'Do you still have the effrontery?' shouted the secretary, nearly beside himself. 'Were it not for the respect that I have for your father…'

'Oh, please!' interrupted the student. 'Leave my father and my mother out of this. I've been weaned for twenty years now. We are only two men here. But so as not to waste any further breath, tell me: are you one of those men who duels?'

'Yes!' Rev. Celzani replied in a loud voice, and he struck a pose that was a bit too melodramatic for the circumstances. 'I am one of those men who fight duels.'

'Well then, that's good enough for me,' said the young man resolutely. 'You will have the honour of seeing me again.' And wheeling around, he went back inside his home.

One hour later, the engineer Ginoni, who had learned everything from Miss Pedani, put on his hat and climbed the stairway in great annoyance in order to go to the secretary and prevent any misfortune that might befall his son. Although he felt truly sorry for the affront that had been made to the young lady, he considered the provocation to have been a youthful folly. But as a man of the world who understood the respect that red-blooded young men give to their own pride, he realised that sheer stubbornness could make them capable of taking things to the very end, and he wanted to arrange everything amicably (short of withdrawing the challenge in his own name), and he hoped to propose a reconciliation that would satisfy both parties.

He presented himself therefore to the secretary alone and in the cordial manner of a friend. However, Celzani, who was very upset and still exceedingly excited by jealousy, received him with great haughtiness (which forced the engineer to work hard to stifle his laughter). Ginoni affably told Rev. Celzani that he had learned of the affair from the young lady and that he had come to work things out on a friendly basis. He deplored the action of his son, but a duel would be folly – a ridiculous absurdity – and discussing it was out of the question. It was necessary to stop the thing at once. 'Come on, my dear secretary,' he said, 'Miss Pedani does not enter into the question. In the name of my son I can offer the most abject apologies in regards to the young lady, as is only fitting. But as far as it concerns you, it was only a little irritation on both sides. All that you have to do is to show a little good will and there the affair will end, I can guarantee it.'

But Rev. Celzani was no longer the Rev. Celzani that he once was. He resisted. 'I have been offended,' he said.

'Come on,' replied the engineer. 'The most serious words that were spoken were "dirty trick", and it was you who spoke them. He who is most reasonable should yield. You are fifteen years older. Blast it, this is not the time to be so pig-headed!'

But the secretary was in a deadly mood because of a certain arm that had extended around a waist. *That* was the problem, not the challenge; it was this that made negotiations difficult.

'Are you suggesting that I swallow my humiliation?' he asked as he grew angrier.

'But what humiliation are you talking about?' exclaimed the engineer. 'That is not the issue. The issue is satisfying the selfish pride of a young man who has issued a challenge. You don't seem to understand. The issue is dealing with the problem in a way that will not result in disaster. You need only say that you are sorry for having said those two words, and I guarantee that it will all be ended. Good God! Is it your stubborn pride or your jealousy that makes you so intractable?'

'Both,' replied Rev. Celzani solemnly.

The engineer looked at him and lost his patience. 'I would not have believed,' he said, hardly able to contain his anger, 'that love had emptied your brain to this extent. Do you therefore seek a duel?'

Celzani raised his head and replied in a truly heroic tone, 'I do not seek it; neither do I fear it.'

'Well then, you should realise that you really are mad,' screamed the engineer in exasperation. 'And if you receive a thrashing, then you deserve it!' And he left, slamming the door violently behind him.

Another tragicomic scene transpired a few hours afterwards on the floor above, and for the same reasons. Miss Pedani had come back home in time for supper, and since she appeared a bit troubled, her flatmate, who was then on speaking terms with her, gently asked her what was the reason. In the past she would not have said a word, but now that she was beginning to feel the need to open her heart, she told her in detail and without caution what had happened and expressed her fears about the eventual results. From the very start, Miss Zibelli was wounded deeply, but she pretended to be unaffected until she had heard the end of the story. But by that time she found that she was speechless – suffocated with rage. Young Ginoni, too! That damnable creature Pedani must have been born to vex her. And who knows how many months this love affair had been going on, for which she had been merely a diversion (perhaps even a stimulus) for a few weeks. She stopped eating and said that she was unwell. She knew that if she did not release her feelings, she would burst, but she could not retain her personal dignity if she exploded on this subject, so with feverish impatience, she searched for another.

Miss Pedani hurriedly finished her supper, and then she opened up an exercise manual by Baumann on the still-set table and began to study the illustrations. Miss Zibelli paced back and forth in the room, biting her lip. Abruptly she stopped behind her friend and glancing at the drawings cried, 'My God, they look like a lot of clowns in those poses!'[38]

When anyone touched on that subject, Miss Pedani reacted instantaneously. She replied, 'Try to find a criticism that is a bit more original if you can. You've been repeating those same words for years.'

'It's because they're still true,' replied Miss Zibelli. 'And I will repeat them until you're deaf so long as you worship some big chief acrobat as if you were a paid member of his troupe.'

It was typical insolence, but Miss Pedani never accepted things for what they were; she had to argue her side of the argument. 'Chief acrobat!' she exclaimed with an ironic smile. 'Baumann has more good sense and talent in his little finger than in all the brains of every Obermann supporter from the past, present and future. End of discussion.'

'Oh, not so fast!' replied Zibelli, shrugging her shoulders. 'Baumann is extremely incoherent, and he makes and un-makes without having a clear and firm view of his method. He would turn the world upside down in order to make himself famous. Nothing more than this!'

'Baumann,' said Miss Pedani quietly, 'has given to Italy a system of gymnastics that it did not have before.'

'How can you say that?' responded Miss Zibelli, 'When he has merely exaggerated everything that had already existed and turned the original into a caricature – it's the easiest thing in the world to do.'

'Oh, that is unfair!' Pedani exclaimed. 'And who first taught (among other things) your precious Obermann about gymnastics done between school benches? And how do you dare to speak for Obermann, who was so progressive and who without a shadow of a doubt would be a devotee of Baumann if he were still alive today, because he had great talent; in the mean time you are not even the guardians of his method – have you not degenerated from his methods?'

Miss Zibelli became livid and ceased all reasoning. 'Well,' she answered, 'even if that is true, it is preferable to your methods, and your gymnastics of sideshow strongmen – dangerous for children, indecent for girls and brutal and exhibitionistic for everyone.'

After her friend gave vent to this outburst, Miss Pedani regained control of herself.

'Well,' she answered flippantly, 'Allow us to break each other's heads, and you can keep your babyish gymnastics. That way you will avoid your "itty-bitty boo-boos" and you can preserve your modesty.'

This caused Miss Zibelli to go off her hinges.

'I refuse to let you make fun of me… on top of everything else,' she cried. 'I'm tired of being insulted. I've taken it long enough. I can't take it any more! I can't take it any more!' And she swept out, slamming the door behind her with all her strength, leaving Miss Pedani sitting there with her manual in front of her, more astonished than offended. But in addition she was wearier than ever of all the reversals and outbursts whose causes she only vaguely suspected. These crises were becoming more frequent and were making it impossible to live together.

Everything went from bad to worse at that time for Rev. Celzani, too. He did not encounter young Ginoni's seconds since the engineer had absolutely forbidden his son to continue the affair. But two days later when he met Mrs Ginoni, who had always been so kind as to allow him to assist her slender and indolent form up the stairs, he was pained to learn that she did not reply to his greetings. He would have been even more offended by this affront if he had known that the good lady had not directed her insult to him because he was her son's challenger but because he had impeded her beloved Alfredo in a gallant conquest, an affair on which she would have been more than happy to wink her maternal eye! That same day he got the *coup de grâce* when he received the same snub from Mr Ginoni, who passed him on the via San Francesco without even turning to look at him. All relations had therefore been broken with the entire family, and this could only add to the morbid excitement of his passion.

Rev. Celzani had to endure other troubles the next day. Among the other girls that came up to the third floor to take private gymnastics lessons was a sort of gipsy with short hair; she was the daughter of a seller of ointments and little soaps who came to Miss Pedani so that she could demonstrate rhythmic gymnastics routines to her; the girl then claimed these as her own personal creations. The child was extremely passionate about gymnastics and a little odd; she was continually trying out new steps everywhere with her skirt pulled up in her hands; she looked like she was afflicted with St Vitus' dance. But the devout ladies on the first floor had twice been startled when they caught the girl on the landing as she was giving a demonstration with her skirts lifted up to another of Miss Pedani's students. Scandalised and furious by this spectacle, they sent for the secretary in order to have him prevent those indecencies, and they told him, 'Because of Miss Pedani, we no longer know what sort of a house this is becoming.' Suffering because of his unrequited love, the secretary was already in a bad mood, and he replied sharply; they rebuked him because of this, and he raised his voice to them. Then they ordered him out while threatening to go to his employer. They forbade him ever to speak to them again.

Even worse was to come the next day. Professor Padalocchi asked him to go to Mr Fassi and ask him in his name to make his children cease jumping about and playing with dumb-bells by a certain hour because it was disturbing his linguistic studies. The secretary was already irritated, so he was not very diplomatic during this mission, and he allowed the word 'racket' to escape from his lips. Fassi became enraged. To call scientific experiments – practical and reasoned preparation that he did for his courses – to call them a 'racket' while he was torturing his brain for the good of humanity, seemed to him to be the ultimate in audacity. And then, backed up by his wife, he attacked the secretary mercilessly, making impertinent allusions to Miss Pedani. Fassi next threatened him and asked him to leave, and then went to complain to the professor. The old man consequently accused Rev. Celzani of having mishandled the case and of having embroiled a professor with an ill-bred lout; he rebuked the secretary, was offended by his answers and never looked him in the face again.

He was thus on bad terms with everyone on that staircase. But it was not over yet. The tenants from the other part of the house had also had reason to complain at that time of his distraction and his irritability, and as word had spread of his falling in love and the change that it had wrought in him, everyone of every social class talked about him without any hesitation. The upshot of their comments was that the stubbornness of this failed priest in running after a girl who did not want him seemed to be a shameless pretension, an indication either of ridiculous pride or even of imbecility. They would not even deign to honour his feeling with the name of love; it could only be the vulgar passion of a former seminarian, and this they could read in his eyes. They spoke of depraved attacks on the girl in the stairway; they considered him a pig, they glared at him. Then they began to do him little discourtesies to which he responded with other discourtesies; these embittered him to the point that he himself became the initiator in this little war. Then several tenants complained in a letter to the commendatore, and several of these mentioned the scandalous love, the shameful persecution from which the girl had suffered, and the scenes in the stairway and in the entryway that had reached the point that mothers of families could no longer leave with their daughters without obliging them to cover their faces with their fans.

They had all done such a good job that one day the commendatore finally lost patience and decided to give his nephew his last notice as soon as he returned for dinner. He did not want to use the harshest words because he was put in a good mood by a letter from Miss Pedani inviting him two days hence to a gymnastics display at the Institute of Military Daughters, where he hoped to find profound subjects of meditation. But he was irritated by the sight of the secretary when he appeared before him, pale and dusty and with his head bandaged. The uncle asked him what had happened to him. The nephew told him. It was at the gymnasium, where he continued to go (although he had lost all hope) in order to calm his nerves, that this had happened. He had begun (out of desperation) an exercise on the balance beam that was too risky; he made a misstep, and he fell down, striking his head against one of the support posts.

The commendatore was equally irritated over what he called this 'buffoonery'. Then with clenched teeth and with a severity that he had never shown him before, he told his nephew that he had had enough of this; he was tired of his negligence, of his disorganised and indecorous life and of the complaints that he had received from many sides. The scandal must come to an end, and if he did not see a radical change in his conduct within the space of one week, he would be sent packing. He already had a replacement in mind. After saying this, he announced that he wanted to dine alone and sat down abruptly.

And then he fell into the lowest depths of despair, which left only one question in his overwrought brain: should he leave for Genoa and then embark for America, or should he stay in Turin and throw away his tiny patrimony in foolishness and debauchery in an attempt to dull the pain and to forget? Either way, he had to leave that house or his life would become intolerable. He packed his bags in silence until it was quite late, then he lay upon the bed completely dressed. But he could not sleep a wink. Suddenly feverish, he listened to the familiar noises for the last time, and that night the noises were continual. The long-awaited teachers' conference had been open for a week, and the debate on gymnastics, during which Miss Pedani had to give her speech, was set to take place on the following day. She was nervous and got out of bed every few moments and then got back in and then got out again; she wandered around the room. He could hear her bare feet. For him this was all the most horrible torture for his senses, but he was dominated by a great feeling of tenderness. He felt a profound regret for having to leave that room forever, for never hearing those familiar sounds again, those noises that he loved by now because they reminded him of so many sleepless nights, so many desires, so many dreams, so much sadness – all things that he would never forget as long as he lived – of that he was sure. He recalled things in the past, and he sat up in bed in order to hear her footsteps and her sighs. He called out to her; he spoke to her; he cried; he bit his fists, and he spent the night like one condemned to death. In the morning he arose tired and battered; his head ached where he had injured it. He was uncertain the entire morning about whether he should say his farewells to her by letter or talk to her in person. He decided to go in person, and at one thirty, he climbed the stairs.

The teacher was alone in the house and a bit sad. After the scene that had been caused by young Ginoni, her friend had made life difficult by a new tactic: it seemed that she wanted to find consolation in food. She wanted to recklessly consume anything that was available; to consume delicacies, to spend lavishly on food that she could ill afford, to gulp everything down like a greedy ostrich. She complained about everything, making dreadful scenes if the sauce was not right, the bread overcooked, the meat too tough, the vinegar too tasteless. Miss Pedani had finally had enough of this. That little viper had even succeeded in poisoning the morning for her at a time when she had such need of tranquillity to prepare her lecture. Stung also by jealousy of her recent triumph, Miss Zibelli had not been able to resist torturing her up to the very last moment, and after having made one of her usual scenes, in which she berated Pedani for being too ambitious and predicted failure, she left without eating.

Miss Pedani was in the parlour in the process of rereading her pages for the last time, already dressed for the programme at the conference, which was to begin at two thirty. She wore a black dress without any trim that moulded to her body as if it were knit, and made her skin look whiter and her stature taller. The agitation of her soul gave to her face an expression of sensitivity that she had never shown before. She was alone, and despite the approach of the hour she looked forward to, when the beautiful golden sun filled the room, she was melancholy. The friends who were coming to fetch her and to give her support had not yet arrived. This solitude weighed heavily on her; she had never desired company so much. She was therefore greatly cheered when the secretary was announced.

He entered with his hat in his hand, noted the black dress and heaved a sigh. With his forehead bandaged, pale, defeated, sad as a funeral mourner, he truly made a pitiable spectacle. He chose not to sit down.

The teacher immediately asked him what had happened to his head.

'Fell at the gymnasium,' he answered. And he added that he had come to say farewell.

Miss Pedani thought that he left every year for the country, and asked him, 'Aren't you even going to the conference?' The secretary had seen his uncle's invitation but had completely forgotten it. Oh well, he would go to the conference first; he would see her once more illuminated by the light of her beauty and her triumph, and then he would go away with that last image before his eyes. But he did not say this, he only thanked her for the invitation that she handed him.

'I'm leaving,' he said with a trembling voice. 'I have come to tell you goodbye – forever.'

The young lady looked at him and understood everything. But she could not find the words to reply to him. What, in fact, could she say to him? She felt that the slightest exhortation to stay would be taken as encouragement, practically as a promise, and her frank nature did not allow her to make any concessions; she could only have done so if she were determined to follow through. She turned her eyes away, embarrassed, and looked towards the window. Then, seeing that his eyes were lowered, she looked at him once more, meditating. She knew everything, and everything returned to her mind at that point. When she had first arrived at that house, he was wise, hard-working, calm, good, and liked by everyone. And everything had fallen apart from there. The first one to be alienated was Miss Zibelli, the teacher Fassi was the next to hate him, the Ginonis had turned their backs and their son wanted to challenge him. Professor Padalocchi no longer spoke to him, the ladies on the first floor had shown him the door, all the tenants were feuding with him, the commendatore wanted to throw him out of the house (and perhaps he already had done so). And now he had to leave alone and homeless. How long did he have to sigh before she noticed it? How he had to suffer disappointment and humiliation; and how he must have loved her to have persisted thus far after so many of her refusals and in spite of everything and at such a terrible cost to himself. And finally, he had even injured his head for her. And she looked at his bandages. And as often happens, it was the comic aspect of this poor bandaged head and the image that it presented as he tumbled off the beam that caused her to pity him, and for the first time to feel a sentiment of tenderness. But poor Rev. Celzani, who could not read her mind, saw only the smile that reflected her final thought but one, and he believed that she was mocking him. That was the final blow.

'Oh,' he exclaimed with a tone of desperate anguish, lifting his eyes and opening his arms, 'You should not do this! I cannot bear the suffering.'

'Mr Celzani, what is it that you think?' asked the young lady as she rushed towards him.

But a chorus of happy voices resonated at that moment in the antechamber, and a laughing squad of teachers dressed in their party finery stormed into the parlour; hardly noticing the secretary they all crowded around their colleague, raising a chorus of greetings and exclamations. They were the friends who had come to accompany Miss Pedani to the conference; they were its passion, its universe, its glory. It was they who tore her from him and who also robbed him of the consolation of a final farewell.

Rev. Celzani gave a last look of adoration – perfectly pure at that instant – at the beautiful creature to whom he would speak nevermore, and choking back his tears, he left unseen.

The conference took place at the Carignano Palace in the hall that had remained intact from the time when it was the Piedmontese parliament. On this day there were perhaps more than three hundred conference-goers and teachers (both men and women) who sat scattered randomly on the velvet upholstered seats, though quite a few of these seats were unoccupied. It was a novel spectacle that took place in this illustrious hall where the voices of the greatest champions of the Italian revolution had resonated in the most terrible and glorious days of our history. It was now occupied by a crowd of elementary schoolteachers who represented in their outward appearances and their fashions of dress all social levels. And yet their presence was not something to laugh at, because it made one realise that the Italian Parliament was very far away, in a city where only a few years earlier it would have seemed impossible to those who were there to imagine it.[39] Above these seats where the Turinese had seen the shine of venerable, hoary heads and the gleam of so many bald-pated legislators, now everywhere rose up the feathers and flowers of the little hats worn by the teachers, scattered about in lines or in groups and who all chirped happily as a flock of little birds. In Garibaldi's sacred seat, there was an old country schoolmaster with a goitre. In the former place of the Count de Cavour there sat a young, beardless man with a carnation in his buttonhole. The president's spot was taken by a fat priest who taught in Naples.

On first glance, one was struck by the variety of physiognomies – after all, this was not a regional conference; rather there were teachers from all the provinces of Italy, among which the dark hair and complexion of the South predominated. On the upper benches were found a large number of young ladies who were variously garbed; these were certificated teachers who were, however, unemployed and who had come as spectators out of curiosity, many of them with sheets of paper in front of them and with pens in hand so as to take notes, and in the middle of this group were boys and girls (their brothers and sisters). Two extremely tall ushers in yellow vests and white stockings walked into the chamber. The gallery was filled with other teachers, parents and conference-goers, and in the first row one could see some of the most illustrious gymnastics authorities in Turin: professors, physicians and representatives of the press. This was the most numerous and vigorously animated assembly that had yet convened at the conference.

When Rev. Celzani entered the ancient public chamber, the programme had been going for nearly an hour. As soon as he was seated, he tried to look for Miss Pedani. He did not find her immediately. He saw Miss Zibelli instead in one of the lowest benches, with her face to the president's dias, sitting among other teachers whom he did not recognise. As he was looking around in the back benches, he came upon the profile of the officious Mr Fassi, who was in the midst of a large group of Turinese gymnastics teachers, nearly all ex-soldiers; among these he recognised the blond head of the teacher from La Generala prison.

But where was she? After having searched at random, he finally found her in one of the highest benches on the right where Massari, Boggio and Lanza, Cavour's most faithful supporters, had sat.[40] She was in a place next to a large window in the middle of the lively crowd of teachers who had come to fetch her from home and who formed a sort of honour guard around her. The sunlight that came in through the big window illuminated the entire right side of her beautiful body clad in the black dress. She had some papers in front of her, and she chatted with her neighbours, but she seemed a bit agitated. The secretary placed one fist atop the other on the ledge and rested his chin on his fists and thus stayed immobile in order to look at her, comforted by a last hope: that she would meet for one last time his gaze when she directed her eyes to his vicinity. This would be the final farewell. Then everything would be over. Nothing else mattered to him. Just as he had upon entering not even looked around that historical chamber that he had never seen before, so he did not hear a single word of the speeches that were being given.

The discussion turned upon a theme that had already been brought up the day before: the opportunity to introduce manual labour sessions in schools. The first to speak was a young teacher from Venice who showed with great gentleness how she had taught her students to make baskets with strips of paper, and samples of her work circulated from hand to hand in the audience where her colleagues attempted to imitate her work. Then it was the turn of an instructor from Calabria who had a sad and musical voice; he showed a large basket of things that were made in his class, among which was even a pair of shoes. After him, several dissenters had taken the floor, and after this the discussion became excited and embittered. A beautiful teacher who was serving as secretary had to reread a part of the record from the other session. On a bench on the extreme left sat a group of young Lombard teachers who were bold and pugnacious, so much so that the president with all of his priestly patience could not succeed in calming their excitement. Two teachers from opposite sides of the chamber exchanged bitter words. In short, a good part of the time was spent on issues of parliamentary procedure, and the speakers must have sensed the political atmosphere that permeated the atmosphere of the hall, for they spoke with too much emphasis, demonstrating an over-excited sense of self-pride.

Rev. Celzani was momentarily distracted by a loud voice that shouted solemnly, 'The representatives of Milan have no imperative mandate.' Then he was jolted once again by a burst of applause in honour of a young teacher who had declared in a soprano voice that if manual labour were adopted in the schools, it would be necessary to increase salaries proportionally. Then followed a new hubbub. Finally, a short and stout teacher re-established calm with a few lucid and reasoned words, and the president could then call for an order of the day and put it to a vote of hands. Two hundred hands shot into the air, among them one could see numerous ladies' gloves buttoned to the elbow; a round of applause followed the vote, and they then passed on to the other point, which was 'Proposed modifications to the teaching of gymnastics'.

The announcement of the subject was a shock to Rev. Celzani, who thought that Miss Pedani would speak immediately. And turning his eyes to the side, he saw appear in the chamber right across from him and directly above Miss Pedani's head, the smiling face of the engineer Ginoni.

His anticipation was disappointed. One teacher after another spoke before her. Right from the start, the discussion meandered in great confusion about the technical aspects of the subject, the point of which seemed to be to display technical phraseology of which the uninitiated could understand nothing. The two schools were being bandied about; the names of Baumann and Obermann were shouted in the middle of a great tumult which was suddenly dominated for a moment by a cavernous voice that declaimed, 'Turin, which was the cradle of gymnastics, will be its grave!'

One teacher attracted the attention of the participants on the need to reform the language of the rules of gymnastics, which were not sufficiently Italian, suggesting that certain issues should be referred to the Academia della Crusca.[41] Rev. Celzani thought that the teacher Fassi might have spoken, and in fact he became excited; he approved this and disapproved that, violently shouting, 'No! Never! That's a bit strong! Have a little sense!' but he did not ask to speak. A gymnastics teacher demonstrated the necessity of improving the condition of his colleagues, who were paid by the government but without many of the rights of other government employees and who found themselves in a precarious state. They were subject to the will of elementary and high-school headmasters who started the courses late, did not allow instructors to participate (as would have been proper) in committees judging exemptions for military service and who granted these almost always according to their whims.

Nor did the authorities back them up in discipline. Then the discussion became confused and heated anew about a methodological controversy in the course of which accents from every part of Italy were heard.

The secretary began to fear that Miss Pedani would never rise to speak, and he prepared himself with great bitterness to give up the final pleasure of hearing her voice, of seeing his idol applauded and honoured, of wearing his glorious despair like the golden rays of a saintly nimbus. Every time a new teacher rose to speak, he was tempted to leave; it seemed to him that she was prolonging his torture on purpose, and he counted the words as he trembled with emotion. Finally, after a brief comment by a Tuscan teacher who caused great applause when she noted, to the great shame of Italy, that little Belgium offered a prize of twenty-five thousand lire to the author of a good book on gymnastics, the president announced in a loud voice, 'Miss Pedani will take the floor.'

Rev. Celzani jumped as if he had been scorched by flames.

At first a low murmur raced through the audience, then there was a great silence which meant that the teacher was known by reputation and that her speech was much anticipated. All eyes turned toward her. As soon as the audience saw her head and shoulders standing tall and majestic before her bench, her beautiful oval face pale but resolute, a new murmur could be heard as the audience commented favourably on her appearance, but this quickly ceased. She caused a second thrill of amazement when everyone first heard the notes of her beautiful and strange voice, almost masculine but harmonious, perfectly in accord with her powerful and slim body.

She began by saying that no improvements could be expected either in the performance of gymnastics or in the condition of teachers, so long as the government in all municipalities as well as all authorities is not made to hear (as they have in other countries) the imperious strength of the nation's voice, which is firmly convinced of the benefits of this instruction and steadfastly determined to have it. The first duty of each person, and of teachers in particular, was therefore to become the defenders of this idea and to inculcate it in the reason, the conscience and the hearts of the people, whatever their social class. She spoke slowly at first, wrinkling her brow as an indication of impatience when the words did not come to her and making an aggressive gesture when she emphasised a phrase as if to rend the veil that enveloped her and to express her concepts no matter what the cost.

'The time has come for gymnastics,' she continued, 'as it has come for many other things in Italy, for example, military instruction in schools. At first there was great enthusiasm for military training, but little by little it was allowed to sink to a state of shameful neglect, and it has ended by causing ridicule to fall upon the concepts of its original proponents. But the fate of gymnastics has been even worse. Against it has been raised an ever-widening army of enemies, and even the school authorities have fallen under its powerful influence, to such an extent that gymnastic instruction tends to become a vain display, a miserable pretence, and even an obvious caricature. Ignorance, the cowardly fear of imaginary dangers, national apathy, the perfidy of certain interested parties who with shameless impudence come to blame gymnastics for the infirmities and organic defects of the young, although it was devised to cure them – all these conspire against gymnastics. And these things would be unbelievable were they were not on view every day.

'The enemies of gymnastics,' she said, 'are the cultured professors who are as debilitated at forty as octogenarians precisely because they have overworked their cerebral systems at the expense of their muscles. The enemies of gymnastics are the mothers of girls who have neither flesh nor blood, future mothers themselves of unfortunate progeny for they have never used their bodies' resources. The enemies of gymnastics are the fathers of young children who because of excessive mental labour fall prey to consumption, contracting terrible mental illnesses, abandoning themselves to hypochondria and the contemplation of suicide! The enemies and the detractors of gymnastics are legion, meanwhile the increasing ease of transportation and the redoubled comforts of modern life tend to make us inactive and easily fatigued, while the vicious struggle for existence every day demands a greater expenditure of strength and health. These are the enemies of gymnastics! Meanwhile we are a pitiful generation, weak and spoiled, destined to fill the hospitals and the hospices with deformity and pain! What blindness! What foolishness! What shame!'

These last words were greeted with a burst of applause. Miss Pedani grew bolder and began to make a comparison between the disrespect and frivolity of gymnastics in Italy with the honour it enjoys in other nearby nations. At this point she committed the error of expanding on statistical quotations, and some signs of opposition began to appear here and there in the chamber. Two or three groups of teachers started whispering among themselves to distract the audience. Rev. Celzani heard Fassi, who never even looked at the speaker, shout out two or three times with irritation, 'This is off the subject! Everyone knows this!' Once he exclaimed so loudly, 'How original!' that many turned to look at him. But eventually

Miss Pedani left behind the statistics and turned to the recent celebrations at Frankfurt, which was much better received. The audience saw for a moment in front of them the great gymnasium overflowing with the flower of German youth and felt the flame of that robust enthusiasm pass above her head. The teacher's face was alight as she used her voice with a powerful sonority and cut the air with her gestures, not excessively, but with the vigour of an inspired priestess. And everyone could sense her whole soul in that sincere eloquence; they could see that her life was consecrated to an idea, a youth that was like a long and austere adolescence, freed of sensuality, repugnant to any sort of sentimental or scholarly affectation. They could tell that she was simple in her habits and in her manners, purified by the constant exercise of her physical strength, which was easily manifested in her flourishing health, her clean spirit and her correct and courageous soul.

And then to finish, she evoked in the chamber the figure of old August Ravenstein, founder of the first gymnasium in his country, who was followed in turn by a procession of the great German gymnasiarchs, benefactors of a million children, whom Germany must thank for its power and its glory.[42] After this, another ovation burst forth that shook both the speaker and the entire assembly, and interrupted her speech for some time. During this time her companions gathered around her, touched her clothing and her hands, and showered her with congratulations.

And then she sprinted to the finish line with increasing good will. Returning to the fundamental matter of her speech, she insisted on the necessity that all teachers had of persuading families as well as teaching the students. This was a task that fell to female teachers more than male because, as they were not able to excel in the discipline and were therefore not suspected of personal ambition, their propaganda would be more effective. 'Let us turn to the mothers,' she said. 'Let us make them see, have them touch with their fingers the wonderful effects of physical education, which are as evident and infallible as the results of an exact science. Let us persuade them that gymnastics is strength and health, and that health and strength are serenity, goodness, courage and greatness of the soul! And if reasoning and example are not enough, let us insist, let us raise the hands of the weak boys and girls with a loving force; let us plead with her because we can save them from illness, from unhappiness and from death. Oh, if only we could fill them with the same indomitable ardour that is within us! And above everything else, we must have faith in ourselves, an ardent and invincible faith that our ideas will one day be everybody's and that a new system of education will remake the world. Yes. I believe what I say just as I believe in the existence of the sun that illuminates us all. A new education founded upon exercises that improve physical strength from infancy and youth will prevent innumerable miseries, free humanity from innumerable pains, cut down a thousand vices at the root and make life easier for new generations, which will be better because they will be stronger, and more just because they will be better. We will find solutions to the great problems against which our sick and exhausted minds now struggle so uselessly. I believe, my dear colleagues, in this new humanity which will raise monuments of bronze to the great apostles of gymnastics. I believe it; I see it; I greet it; I venerate it and I would like for all to consider it as the holiest of human glories to live and die for.'

This conclusion unleashed a storm of applause; everyone jumped up, clapping their hands and shouting; Miss Pedani, pale and breathless, had to rise three times to acknowledge the ovations. The last words had truly been said with the vigour of apostolic enthusiasm, and everyone had been deeply touched. Just when the applause was on the point of ending, it began again; all the proponents of gymnastics on the floor and in the galleries were enraptured. Two or three speakers who came later were hardly heard. When the session was ended, new ovations broke out, and Miss Pedani left her seat between two rows of smiling faces and proffered hands in the midst of a deafening tumult of congratulations and hurrahs.

The image of a human creature enjoying his last delirious hours on the threshold of an enchanted castle, just before he falls through a trapdoor and into an eternal prison, would give a feeble idea of the poor secretary's state of mind after he had heard the speech and the applause and seen the teacher's figure illuminated little by little and becoming almost gigantic. When she had finished, he looked around him as if he had emerged from a dream and he suddenly felt such a wave of sadness and self-pity that it took some effort to hold back his tears.

At this point, he heard a familiar voice calling him. 'Mr Celzani!' He turned and saw the thousand smiling wrinkles of the Cavaliere Pruzzi, still vibrant with enthusiasm under his wig, which lay crosswise. 'Did you hear, eh?' he said, sticking out his round belly. 'What teachers we have in Turin! It cannot be said that the municipal government wastes its money!' And then, either because of the effects of enthusiasm or because he was beginning to repent his calculated reticence when on that memorable occasion he had kept the secretary on tenterhooks and thrown a mysterious veil over the girl, he began to pour out a barrel of praise, and as he did so he held on to the back of

Rev. Celzani's collar, since the latter wanted only to leave. He said that he had not been up to date for very long on Miss Pedani's past. She had a long list of distinctions in her file. She had rendered a singular service to the superintendent of Milan by intrepidly resisting the entire population of a village that did not want her after she had been appointed by the government, and because of this they forced her to leave. She returned under the protection of a company of artillerymen, and she remained in her place with admirable steadfastness after they were withdrawn. She had distinguished herself by fighting a fire in the town of Camina,[43] and in this same town she had saved a child from drowning in a stream and thereby earned for herself an honourable mention on the list of civil valour. 'So what do you think of that?' he asked after catching his breath. 'Now she has brought honour to Turin – good heavens, what am I saying – to all of Italy. We have concerns, that is true, we have great responsibilities, but sometimes we are compensated.' And he added, turning towards the hall, which was already nearly empty, 'Brava, brava and brava again!'

But the secretary paid little attention to him and left him abruptly. He walked down the stairs half in a daze. In the foyer he came upon a crowd that was circling around someone, and guessing that Miss Pedani was in the middle of it, he approached. Indeed, it was her, surrounded and being congratulated; he recognised the green feather of her little hat.

As he was going up on tiptoes to see her face, he heard the voice of Fassi coming from behind him, and when he turned around, he saw him declaiming in a group with reddened face, furiously twisting the ends of his long moustaches. 'In conclusion,' he said, 'she has done nothing more than to run around in circles. Superb quotations, great rhetoric, but where is the science?' And he accused her of plagiarism. 'As for the ideas, well let us pass over them,' he shouted, 'but the sentences, the very words, she has stolen them from me without bothering to mention my name, but I can quote you the words one after the other, and you will see that it is as if they had been taken down in shorthand. Good lord, what brass! Be careful what you say in a casual conversation! And now she's on her way to a brilliant career. You'll hear a lot of blather from those idiot journalists! Oh, what charlatans they all are!'

In the meantime, Miss Pedani attempted to clear a path. When the crowd of her admirers had become a little thinner, Mr Ginoni rushed in near her, and said to her while taking her hands, 'Sublime! You have nearly converted me. I will only say that.' Then the Cavaliere Padalocchi shuffled forwards to congratulate her. Then it was the turn of the director. It still was not over. Only about twenty teachers remained around her, while a great number looked at her from afar; then, the secretary could finally see her without fear of being seen. To him she had never seemed so beautiful, so resplendent, so superb! Her entire body seemed to tremble in that simple black dress, as if a wave ran through her from head to foot. The colour had returned to her cheeks: that beautiful, delicate and diffused blush that comes after the paleness of great, pleasant emotions like the well-deserved joy of glory. Her face wore an expression of gentle, feminine goodness that Celzani had never seen before and which gave to her eyes and to her mouth and to her entire body a new seductive strength. And he looked at her ecstatically, filled with a strange and sad feeling as if he were already very far from her, on the other side of an immense river, on the summit of a hill behind which she had disappeared forever.

When she began to leave surrounded by her faithful escorts, the secretary hid behind a pillar, and from there he witnessed an unexpected scene. Just at the moment when Miss Pedani was to walk out the door, Miss Zibelli appeared before her and threw her arms around her neck weeping and ardently kissed her several times. Rev. Celzani did not hear what she said, but he understood vaguely that she had been defeated and that she had come, moved by an impulse of the heart, to throw down her weapons and ask for forgiveness for something. Miss Pedani kissed her, and her friend went away quickly, but as she turned, she gave an emotion-filled wave of her hand.

Then she went out into the street, and he followed at a respectful distance.

At first she walked slowly, preceded, flanked and followed by a crowd of young teachers, the usual satellites of the victors who made a cheerful chatter around her, warning her to avoid the carriages and casting glances here and there as if to attract the attention of passers-by. Every now and then one of them dropped out and another arrived and joined the group. They arrived at the via Santa Teresa, and they all turned right and continued on their way with poor Rev. Celzani still following.

Yes, he wanted to see her as soon as possible; then he would gather up his things and leave Turin. To go where? He did not know. To Genoa perhaps, from where he could go abroad. He would be guided by God. To go far away, to suffocate his passion in a life of hard work, to forget, or if that were not possible, to suffer less. Since, truly, his moral strength would not permit him to confront further the desperate life that was now his. And after this triumph, he felt more miserable and, so to speak, more desperately unhappy than he had ever been because in the past he had seen nothing else but the external differences between them, but now he realised that she was much superior to him even in the realm of the spirit. While she had ascended to glorious heights, he had been cast down into the dust. He imagined her a few years hence, famous, sought after by all, perhaps married to a handsome, illustrious and powerful man. It seemed to him that it was sheer folly that he had dared to ask for her hand, to trouble her to kneel in front of her and to embrace her knees. This memory of that embrace, or rather the feelings that it reawakened in him, set his blood and his brain alight. And meanwhile, he devoured her from afar with his eyes.

She was hidden from him sometimes by a carriage, at other times by a group of people, but then she would reappear, and each time she seemed to him greater, more beautiful, more triumphant, and each time a spike of despair was driven deeper into his lacerated heart.

Her friends accompanied her all the way to the door. He stopped at the corner of the via San Francesco. From there he waited to see her disappear forever as if into an abyss. But then he saw her friends leave her, and she entered the house. A sudden, uncontrollable need impelled him to say farewell for the last time.

He ran across the road, entered the courtyard and went behind a pillar; from there he saw her go towards the interior door and climb the steps slowly, turning back every now and then as if she had lost her way or missed the company that had left her – or as if after the brilliant triumph in the midst of a crowd, she greatly disliked to return home all alone and to climb that black and solitary stairway.

He followed her on tiptoe, very softly. When she arrived at the second floor, he could not restrain himself; he proceeded and caught up with her. She turned to him and they found themselves face to face in the darkness; she was on the upper step.

'Mr Celzani?' inquired the teacher.

He sighed and murmured, 'I have come to say goodbye!'

But he had not finished his words when he felt a powerful hand on the nape of his neck and two fiery lips on his mouth; and in the delirious joy that invaded him in the midst of that immense dark paradise, where he felt himself lifted up as if by a whirlwind, he could only emit a strangled cry: 'Oh! Great God!'

1. In the years after unification, there were many journals founded to promote and spread interest in gymnastics. *New Arena* (*Nuovo Agone*) was one of these.

2. Emilio Baumann (1843–1916) was the great 'gymnasiarch' and administrator of Italian gymnastics in its earliest years. He was particularly interested in forming a uniquely Italian system of exercise to differentiate it from the systems of Germany, France and Great Britain, and in 1866 he published *La Ginnastica Italiana* in which he tried to make gymnastics less military in their intent and more suited to use in schools.

3. *Commendatore* is an honorific title that was given to men who were prominent in public or private life.
Vanchiglia is a working-class suburb of Turin.

4. The title 'don' is used by De Amicis most often when referring to young Celzani. In the north this term is usually applied to clergymen. I have chosen to use the English title 'reverend' as the best approximation of the term.
It is interesting to note that the author uses very few first names in this work.

5. '*Larga di spalle e stretta di cintura*' ('wide of shoulders and narrow of waist') is a quote from Venetian playwright Carlo Goldoni's play *Il maestro di ballo* (*The Dancing Master*).

6. The Turin Gymnasium refers to the 'Royal Gymnastics Society' on the via Magenta.

7. This refers to the Scuola Elementare Margherita di Savoia.

8. The honorific title 'Cavaliere' is conferred on those who are distinguished for their work in certain fields.

9. See the Introduction for an explication of these two gymnastic schools. Turin was the site of the Great Gymnastics Congress on several occasions between 1877 and 1898.

10. Francesco De Sanctis (1817–83) was responsible for founding in 1878 a school for gymnastics educators in Turin, and afterwards it was at his urging that gymnastics became obligatory in Italian schools.

11. These are all schools for girls in Turin. The 'Gymnasium' referred to in the sentence is the Royal Gymnastics Society.

12. A dynamometer is a calibrated instrument used to measure muscular strength, usually grip strength. Dr Baumann had modified the device so as to measure the changes in the body's weight during movement.

13. Émile Augier (1820–89) was a French playwright who described the social life, problems and manners of the bourgeoisie.

14. Otto Heinrich Jäger developed a heavy iron wand or stick that was used by gymnasts to develop their muscles.

15. The original is '*Che non può un'alma ardita / Se in forti membra ha vita?*' and it is found in the *Ode to Education* by Giuseppe Parini (1729–99).

16. Pietro Gallo was a co-founder of the National Federation of Gymnastics in 1869. Giovanni Battista Bizzarri (not Pizzarri as his name appears in the novel) was active

in getting Italian soldiers into adequate physical shape. The misspelling of his name originated with De Amicis and was not corrected in subsequent editions of the novel. Francesco Ravano was an editor of the pioneering journal *La Ginnastica*. Ravenstein published several articles in *La Ginnastica* urging instructors to use originality in their teaching methods. Ida Lewis (1842–1911) was a heroic female lighthouse keeper in Rhode Island who was officially credited with saving eighty-one lives over the course of her 39-year career at Lime Rock.

17. Dr Giovanni Orsolato was awarded a first prize in the 'teacher's section' at the sixth Gymnastics Congress in Siena in 1875.

18. Choreographic (or rhythmic) gymnastics was an offshoot of the system devised by François Delsarte, a French vocal and dramatic teacher who thought that the best poses and gestures necessary in singing and acting could be learned from physical exercises.

19. The Società Filotecnica of Turin was founded in 1879 to promote scientific knowledge.

20. Aristodemus Malacus (the effeminate) was tyrant of Cumae in the late sixth and early fifth centuries BC.

21. The engineer actually exclaims in French, 'Jamais de la vie!' Most educated Turinese spoke French as well as Italian.

22. The Gymnastics Congress (or Turnfest) at Frankfurt am Main took place on 25th–28th July 1880, and was a landmark in world gymnastics competition because of the international nature of the event and the great crowds that were attracted. Friedrich Ludwig Jahn (1778–1852) was a Prussian gymnastics director and patriot who was known as *Das Turnvater*, 'The Father of Gymnastics'. He used his system of training to inspire patriotism in Prussian youth and to make gymnastics available to all social classes.

23. Like seeks like.

24. This statement reveals more about Mrs Fassi's ignorance than it does Miss Pedani's. '*Il nervo della simpatia*' or sympathetic nerves originate in the lumbar or thoracic region of the spinal cord, and they regulate certain muscular movements. Mrs Fassi obviously confused the meaning and assumed that Pedani was asking about 'the love nerve' or something of that sort.

25. The dashing Bersagliere, or light-artillery units, were renowned for their rakish hats, each sporting 400 black cock feathers, and for the stirring trumpet fanfares that accompanied their quick marches.

26. The Istituto di Soccorso was an organisation founded to help those in financial or medical need.

27. The 'sezione Savoia' was a school district in Turin. It was named for Piedmont's ruling family, the Casa di Savoia.

28. Nueva Granada comprised what is now Colombia and Panama.

29. *La ginnastica fra i banchi* (gymnastics among the school desks) was a system first devised by Emilio Baumann in 1870 so that students would be able to do some exercises while confined to their desks. Although even the author admitted that this method was not the best, for some Italian school children it was the only organised physical education that they ever got.

30. Sybaris was an ancient Greek city in southern Italy. Its citizens were said to be addicted to luxury and pleasures of the flesh. The city was destroyed in 510 BC.

31. Per Henrik Ling (1776–1851) was a Swedish gymnastics teacher who believed that movement was like thought for the body, but just as thoughts need to be in a specific order and to proceed from premises, so movements need to be rational. Unlike Jahn or Obermann, Ling wanted to make the individual stronger and more whole, not necessarily to create stronger and better soldiers.

32. The first of these quotes is by Count Giacomo Leopardi (1798–1837) and is found in his work *Aspasia*. The great Italian poet and librettist Metastasio (1698–1782) wrote the second of these two fragments.

33. Piazza Solferino is a lovely (though busy) area of Turin. It is surrounded by nineteenth-century buildings including Palazzo Ceriana, designed by Carlo Ceppi. Fancy restaurants (such as the Café Monviso) and the Alfieri Theatre surround the piazza.

34. Guido Baccelli (1832–1916) first became minister of education in January 1881.

35. The 'Little House of Divine Providence' at Cottolegno was (and still is) a charitable institution ministering to those suffering from physical and mental problems.

36. This is an energetic ancient dance practised by Spartan and Athenian warriors.

37. Growing as it goes along.

38. The great rivalry between Baumann and Obermann was fought on many planes in Italian society. Basically, Obermann was the founder of 'military gymnastics' which were seen as more Germanic in content, while Baumann was the champion of the more nationalistic 'Italian' gymnastics. Obermann advocated using apparatus while Baumann preferred 'natural' exercises such as walking, marching, climbing and jumping. See the Introduction for a fuller explanation of this conflict.

39. At the time of the story, the Italian Parliament met in Rome (the 'very distant city'), but this had not been possible until 1870. In that year the Papal forces were defeated and the peninsula was united at long last. The dream of Rome as the capital of a united Italy was the long-sought and hard-won dream that only a few years earlier had seemed impossible.

40. Giuseppe Massari (1821–84), Pier Carlo Boggio (1827–66), Giovanni Lanza (1810–82). By placing Miss Pedani among the great nationalists and patriots of the Risorgimento, De Amicis is emphasising the importance that physical education has to play in Italian life.

41. The Accademia della Crusca was founded in Florence in order to safeguard the purity of the Italian language, much like the Académie française in France.

42. August Ravenstein (1809–81) was very active in the German Turner movement and was greatly admired by Rudolfo Obermann.

43. Camina is a community located between Bologna and Imola in Emilia-Romagna.